DESERT FOX BY THE SEA

by Christine Sloan Stoddard

Typeset in Sentinel
Printed in the United States of America
by Biltmore Pro Print

Managing Editor and Copy Editor, Jared Duran
Cover Art by Christine Sloan Stoddard
Book Design by Janell Hughes

ISBN 978-1-7323361-9-3
Library of Congress Control Number: 2018968604

first edition
10 9 8 7 6 5 4 3 2 1

Published by Hoot n Waddle
Phoenix, AZ

hootnwaddle.com

This book is for the woman who thought she'd die of thirst all those times, but didn't.

Hoot n Waddle
Phoenix, AZ

The Re-Coupling

I did not lose the baby—she died. There was never any question about where she was. First, she was inside of me and then she was in the toilet. She didn't hide. She didn't run away. I never had to phone a search party. When she called my womb home, I felt her. When my body expelled her like poison, I saw her. I always knew exactly where she was.

We did not try again for a year because that meant putting his cock where she had been last. Trying again would mean replacing her and I was still sorting out what had happened. One day, I was pregnant and the next day, I wasn't. I couldn't figure out the cause, only the effect.

He said I would be my normal self again if only I said yes. But I kept saying no, and soon he was the one who would break down sobbing because blue-veined cheeses go with gin and stout, didn't I know that? Or the lint roller belongs in the top left drawer, so why was I putting it in the top right?

The first time we embraced in all those months was right after I downed too much Moscato because I had grown cheap and childish. Even though his first thrust was hesitant and shy, I thought he had punched my cervix. When I squirmed, he dotted my forehead with kisses and I froze. The next thrust was faster, bolder. Each thrust went harder, deeper. A voice told me to lunge for his neck, so I heeded the call and bit him like in the old days before she died. He bit me back. At one point, we established a rhythm, an understanding. The last thing I remember before falling asleep was suppressing a tiny burp that tasted like semen and sweet wine.

Jaguar in the Cotton Field

One month after my mother's mother was raped with a knife,
she crawled into the coffin that was her kitchen,
drenched herself in kerosene,
and lit her flesh on fire.

Like the man in the park where the saguaros grow,
the flames made my grandmother pray for death,
but death was the jaguar in the cotton field
that fate forbade her from catching.

Fate eventually exercised mercy
when she died in the hospital one week later,
with the spotted pelt in her hands at last.

Though I never knew her, I visit her grave every Sunday
to pay homage to a woman's pain,
to the ever-shrinking smallness she felt in the world,
to the smallness I myself know.

Requiem for a Twin

A pall has been cast over your layette. I sit on the edge of the bathtub, naked. The double stroller must go up in flames. I rub my globular belly, wishing I had a map to find you. Burn half of the blankets, the bibs, the binkies.

When the ultrasound revealed not one, but two, I cried. Twice the bundle, twice the joy. Always two armfuls of fat rolls, gurgles, and heartbeats.

The nursery became a shrine to the unborn as I bought, unpacked, piled, and arranged. Meanwhile, I grew and stretched and ached.

Then your heart stopped. And my aches multiplied.

They said your sister lived. But you had vanished:

"A fairly common chromosomal syndrome."

Though my body may have absorbed you, I have not absorbed my grief. Every night, I bathe almost to dehydration.

When your sister comes into this world, the loss of you will be final, my child.

Thoughts on a Winter Morning Walk through Manhattan, by Myself, as a Woman

Today, I put on the old, brown boots that finally gave out. And there's not a shoe shop anywhere in the city open at this hour. I'll stop in here to dry off, warm up.

Wow, this deli looks and smells like it really has been around since 1976.

So, this is where the cops eat. At least it's cheap. Oh, and fast. There's my greasy panini. Western omelet with cheese.

There could've been a better way to start this morning than switching Megabuses in a snowy Elizabethtown parking lot at 4 a.m.

Why do I put myself in bizarre, uncomfortable, lonely situations when traveling?

At least I got my panini now. I love it when the cleaning guy mops while you're eating.

Whoa. How can anyone drink coffee this hot? Nobody ever believes I want black coffee, either. "Not a little sugar?" No, or I would've asked. Women with little girl voices can like black coffee, too, ya know.

Great, hair and skin infomercials. Just what I need when I look like a drenched rat. Look away from the perfect pores.

A sign on the wall says "CPR kit located at manager's desk." What? By the time you read that, it'll probably be too late.

Okay, that was good. I'm outta here.

Why does New York have so many creepy basements? Hey, is that shop open? Yes, please and thank you.

The comfiest shoes in the world are waterproof work boots. Men's. Round-toe. Dorktastic but guaranteed to keep your feet from getting soggy. The best $40 I ever spent. Now where the heck is the subway? Maybe I'll just wander until I find it.

That man coming toward me is definitely going to rape me. I knew this wasn't going to be my day, but, hey, if you can survive here, you can survive anywhere.

Mestiza Girl

I was not the blood cot
in the gurgling toilet
that my mother mistook
for a miscarriage.
I am the tangle of tissue,
a woman-star in the
constellation of humanity.
Mother had lived 40 years
on this planet
when I became the
miracle in her womb.
When the quickening came
on Columbia's campus,
she dropped her books
and prayed for my health
and joy as much as she prayed
for my beauty to take after
my father's blond locks
and bright alabaster skin,
a beauty drained of color.

Origin of a Mermaid

A mother heaving
    on the operating table,
        the siren washed ashore,
          fileted in half.
The doctors cut her
    with their human knives
    and human words.
She flows and flows,
    her siren blood,
    her siren flesh.

She hears the ocean
    as she pushes,
      as she grits her shark-like teeth.

In her fever dream,
    she imagines it is raining pearls.

When will her minnow swim into this world?
    The air thickens with a sea breeze
      the longer she labors.

Gulls cry.
    Whales moan.

Crabs stir the sand up into song.

All manner of marine life
    beckon this small creature
      onto land.

The shore may seem perilous for a mermaid,
    But the water promises no refuge:
      Half-woman.
      Half-fish.
        She belongs
        and does not belong
        wherever she ventures.

The little mermaid finally emerges
    from her mother's womb
      hesitantly,
      as much as she might emerge from
      coral forests in coming months,
      wary of prowling squids
      and scuba men with spears.

The mother mermaid cradles her newborn
    and serenades her with that voice

sailors know and love and fear.

Welcome to the world, little mermaid.
    Learn to swim fast.
    Learn to question fast.
    Do not startle fast.
    Do not trust fast.
You can control no one but yourself
    and the Moon controls us all.

Twenty-Six

I am the age my mother was when she killed herself—to the month, to the week, to the day.

Everyone says I could've been her twin because I look just like her. I say I might as well have been her twin because she never saw me as her daughter. Instead, I was a perpetual nuisance.

I can still hear her Lauren Bacall voice snapping at me as I toddled about:

"Put your stupid bear away. You're too old for it."

"That's not a boo-boo. It's a scratch. Use real words, and stop crying."

"Go to your room and don't come out until you're ready to fix yourself dinner."

My mother never wanted to be a mother—mine or anyone else's. She feared the stretch marks, the changed breasts, the torn vagina. Her dread of lost freedom came second.

"I haven't gotten my nails done since before you were born," she used to say. "You turned me into a regular frump."

Nobody knew she was a frump but her.

My mother was the kind of beautiful people noticed: tall but not too tall, slender yet curvy, long-haired, clear-faced, bright-eyed. She had dropped out of high school to become a trade show model, working until she met my father on the hood of a Jaguar. Oiled from head to toe, she wore a leopard-print bikini. My balding father wore a gray suit and carried a briefcase. He bought the car right then and there. Then he asked my mother to go for a ride with him. I came three months into their marriage.

Sometimes, when I was supposed to be sleeping, I'd watch my mother wallow before her vanity as I hid in the closet. She'd dip her fingers into various jars, smear lotions on her face, and study her reflection before wiping her face clean. Then, sulking, she would slip into her cold bed. My father was never home those nights, and I didn't dare move until I was sure she had fallen asleep. Cuddling was forbidden.

When I study my reflection now, I see my mother. Perhaps I am a few pounds heavier. Perhaps I am more prone to smiling. But it wasn't just sheer luck that, throughout my teens, when I showed people pictures of her, they believed I modeled on the weekend.

The main difference is that I will not run the hot water. I will not smash the mirror and take a shard into the tub. I will not sing, "Down the road, the long, long road," as my baby plays House in the den. I will not paint the bathroom tile red as I leak to death.

I will put on my clothes and go to the den and pick up the baby and hold her tight. Then I will put her down and show her how to tie an apron and cut a cake and eat a slice.

This is our house—the same house where my mother lived at my age. But by tomorrow, I will be older than she ever was.

Separate Stars

We are burning
in the amber sky,
pinned up over
Manhattan skyscrapers,
one brighter,
one dimmer,
yet sewn into
the same constellation.

My mother breathes
into my mouth
so I can swallow
her sparkles.

I stopped holding
Mother's hand
the first time
a Park Avenue woman
asked if
she was my nanny.
Today, I would beckon
her into a black hole.

Mother and I have

built a universe.
We cut our
silhouettes out
from dusky velvet
because silhouettes
are all the same color.

Twinkle, Star Mama.
Twinkle, and I will
watch and learn.

Never Been Born

Bullets and bloodshed raised a generation
    of Salvadoran boys and girls
    in mud and tears,
but my mother remembers racing through
      pristine coffee plantations
      & sucking the red flesh off bulging beans
    before machine guns conquered los ranchos,
    before killing begat killing,
    because there is momentum in murder.

And then there was slaughter.
And then she was grown.
And there was still slaughter.
But she was grown & you cannot *un*grow,
just as you cannot *un*see
the blood,
    the bodies,
      the blood,
        the bodies,
          the blood,
            the bodies,

She was grown, so she fell in love
    with an American photographer

in El Salvador to capture the blood and bodies.
Under her love, he flourished
    like the coffee plants of her childhood,
    tiny Christmas trees in the black earth.

When my father was called to the United States,
    he would not leave her
    to be murdered somewhere en la calle or an indigo field,
so they cried over immigration papers and prayed
    and waited,
    and prayed,
    and waited,
    and prayed
until my mother was accepted.

But that was three decades ago,
    three decades before Trump
Today I never would have been born

Today my mother would be buried
    in San Salvador.

Procreation's Truth

Growing a fetus requires no love,
only a viable container.
See, it's not love.
It's science.

That's why I'm here:
My mother's uterus
accepted me.
Her heart did not.
My father's heart
accepted me
even less.

I can only hope
that God loves me
because Abuela is
but a ghost
and ghosts cannot love.

Love is for the living.

My Nightingale

There's an Old World flycatcher sleeping in my throat. The slow song of a dark spell destined her to eternal slumber. Better off dead than dormant, I say, and yet the thrush lives.

A lover once set a ruby rose afloat on a little boat to wake her. He was the lover of a lifetime, and yet the feckless thrush lives. No rose—no matter how red or fragrant—could wake her.

I dream of my nightingale opening her eyes and her beak, and singing my story to a public that would never hear me.

She would explain the scars, the tears, and the many moons spent curled up on the kitchen floor, scratching my ankles with fingernails shredded from teeth always gnashing or grinding.

Luna

I snuck out of the diner, clutching the banana milkshake I should not have ordered. *It has fruit in it,* that devilish little voice inside my head reasoned. *Besides, it's what I ate the night I lost my virginity. It's healthy* and *nostalgic.* Before the internal debate could continue, a battered Luna moth crashed into my shoulder. Startled, I backed up into the diner door and nearly sent my shameful shake tumbling to the ground. I caught the cup before spinning around in search of the moth. The humongous insect was busy pumping its lime-green wings, only to suddenly plummet toward the ground. Before it could hit the pavement, the moth darted back and forth and attempted another ascent. I popped the milkshake straw into my mouth and watched it struggle until it stopped moving at all. I remembered reading that Luna moths only lived four days. Under the red and yellow flood of the diner light, it occurred to me that the moth might be dying.

This was not the first time I bore testament to a creature's death. When I was five, I ran over a mauled mouse with my bicycle. I saw it bleeding out on the sidewalk and wondered if it was a Halloween prop. The pitiful squeak and crack of breaking bones that followed my test assured me that it was not. As further proof, my glittery pink training wheels turned crimson. I didn't cry, though I did feel compelled to bury the mouse. My cat, Lola, whisked away the tiny corpse before I could dig a grave. When I was eight, my 10-year-old neighbor, Garrett, snapped a sparrow's neck in front of me. He said he could bring it back to life. That was a lie. Prior to that episode, I thought I would marry Garrett. I fell out of love with him almost as quickly as I fell in love with him. Four years after I buried that sparrow in my grandmother's garden, Nana died, but I did not witness her death. I witnessed my mother's.

Nana breathed her last breath buried under a pile of books in bed. Judging by what was open on her chest when I found her, she had been reading *Anna Karenina*. I knew it was not the first time, but it was certainly the last. I closed the book and then her eyelids. They were cold and papery. I had never noticed how long her eyelashes were before that moment. After staring at Nana long enough, I picked up the phone. I called the police before I thought to call Mom. Once I hung up, I curled up at Nana's feet for a spell before dialing Mom. I wanted to absorb all of Nana's peace and happiness and goodwill. She still smelled like old books and butterscotch.

Eventually, I called Mom because I did not know where she was. If I was lucky, she hadn't dropped another prepaid cell phone into a porta potty bowl. She was not in Nana's house and I knew she wasn't at our apartment because I had the only key. She lost her copy and I would not let her in the house until she stopped taking Oxy. Though she said had quit, I knew she was lying. By age 12, I had learned to recognize addiction. Mom was my textbook. Undeterred by my stubbornness, Mom slept on the back steps. I didn't feel too bad because it was summertime. It was actually cooler outside than in our ancient apartment. Air conditioning was another luxury we forewent. Sometimes it stormed, but a roof kept Mom dry. Most nights were so clear that you would fall asleep before you could count all of the stars in sight. When Mom asked about the bathroom, I told her she had to use the women's restroom at the public library and bathe at the YWCA until she got clean. That's what we had done during the many times Mom lost her house keys when I was little. She took my advice on the public library, but didn't bother with the latter. Her punishment had been going on two weeks when I stumbled across Nana in bed with Tolstoy.

Mom sometimes worked for a woman who lived three blocks down from us. She did odd jobs for the properties Mrs. Shelley managed. But I doubted she was there. It was already dinnertime. Besides, we hadn't had enough money for groceries for three weeks, which is why I had gone to Nana's house in the first place. I was hungry. Anytime I was hungry and had no money of my own, I could go to Nana and ask for food. The only problem was that I had to ride a bus to get there. Nana could not drive. It was a bumpy, hour-long ride through places I would have never walked alone. Block after block of boarded up houses haunted me. I imagined them filled with cobwebs and skeletons. None of the yards had grass. Few souls wandered through the area by foot. The ones who did scuttled like spiders escaping a persistent crow.

I still don't know where Mom spent her time before she rolled up to our apartment steps. I was usually working odd jobs myself. I walked dogs, fed cats, watered plants, collected mail, checked in on younger kids who were home alone, and did whatever else neighbors thought a determined 12-year-old girl could handle. They paid me in cash and I hid every dollar from Mom. I squirreled away money for the essentials—mainly bus fare, some food, and a dent on the house phone bill. I did these things instead of daydreaming and going to slumber parties. I did these things because Mom was a drug addict and I loved her, but I could not rely on her. I couldn't even rely on her to be anywhere at any particular time.

I left Nana's house before the police could arrive. I wanted to avoid talking to a social worker with hot breath and a furrowed brow. The last time I spoke to a social worker was when I was five years old. My father had just beaten Mom again, but it was the first time I called 911. When the operator asked what was wrong, I said, "Daddy hit Mommy and she's bleeding on the floor like she's going to die." That night was the last time I saw my father. Then we moved 500 miles south to the town where Nana lived, just one town away from where Mom grew up. We didn't live with Nana because Mom thought it would be too easy for Dad to find us. So she changed her name and rented an apartment on the other end of town. It was a 20-minute drive or an hour by bus. Sometimes, we had a car. Sometimes, we didn't. Mom used to say that at least we had each other. That was until we didn't.

I dashed onto the bus just as a storm rattled the sky. I took my seat and leaned my head against the window. As rain hit the glass like bullets, I thought of Nana. She had been the only adult I ever trusted. Now all I had of her was the scent of her butterscotch lotion on my shirt. When the bus reached the last block before my stop, I prayed that Mom was on the back steps. That was the one prayer that God answered all night. I splashed through fat puddles to our apartment. I burst through the front door and then the back door. Mom was there, barely sheltered from the downpour. Her eyes, usually two black moons, had pinpoints for pupils and her lips had turned blue. She remained silent, even after I shook her. Then her eyelids sagged closed. I took her into my arms, feeling her heart beat like she was trapped underwater in a prehistoric era. Her skin was slick with cold sweat. Her faint, slow breaths tickled my neck as I squeezed her. I froze, just holding her because I wanted to believe she would wake up. Before long, her heart stopped beating at all. I pretended she was asleep until my body gave in from exhaustion.

I woke up to Lola licking my face. It was morning and the yard was still muddy from yesterday's storm. I could smell the earthworms rushing above ground. I could also smell Mom, who was crushing my legs. I pushed her off of my thighs until I remembered she was dead. I jumped back and wrung my hands as I looked at her body in its awkward pile. She was heavier than I thought. How would I move her? With all of my weight, apparently. With a few shoves, I set Mom flat on the landing. I gazed upon her gray-blue face for a minute before I burst into tears. Lola pushed into me as if to say, "Clutch me while you sob." That's exactly what I did. She purred like the ocean in a conch shell.

When Lola stopped purring and glanced up at me, I got up and went to the kitchen. I had to call 911, even though I knew it meant foster care. It all happened so quickly that I barely remember Mom's funeral. I mostly remember wearing shoes that my foster mother, Nancy, gave me. They were patent leather Mary Janes designed for a girl half my age. I hated how childish they made me look. For the remainder of our relationship, she would always treat me like a child, as if she had forgotten that I witnessed my mother's death.

In dreams, I saved Mom faster than a shooting star. I wouldn't have resorted to any of the mythological treatments. No shoving her under an ice-cold shower or pouring coffee down her throat. Instead, I called 911 immediately or, better yet, I already had naloxone on me and knew exactly how to use it. Mom bolted up and never touched Oxy again. A fairy tale ending. But that's not what happened in real life and I had to live with that fact. I tried to drown it with bourbon on the one-year anniversary of Mom's death. Nancy never locked up her liquor. That knowledge defined my adolescence. When you are drunk more often than you are sober, you lose your grasp on time. All you want is your next drink. You float like a butterfly in search of flowers because flowers are all that matter. Flowers dull the pain.

Standing outside the diner, I couldn't watch the Luna moth anymore. I put my milkshake on the window ledge and used both hands to lift the big-winged splendor from the ground. I could feel life pulsing through it, however faintly. Slowly, I raised my arms toward the sky and waited for the moth to move. First, it tapped its toes. Then it fluttered its wings but not hard enough to leave my palms. It tried again and again until it propelled itself into the night sky. It glowed as it flew. I watched it soar until it faded into the stars. I wanted that moth to be Mom. I settled for the moth saying hello to Mom for me on its way home. I just had to decide which star in the sky was Mom. I wanted it to sparkle bright without being the brightest star, or else someone else might have already chosen it for their loved one. I needed to be able to find it again, too. The sky shimmered with possibilities. After choosing Mom's star, I whispered the message I wanted the moth to relay. Then I picked up my banana milkshake and took a sip. The flavor was as sweet and full as I needed it to be.

Ave Creole Madonna

Draw an "X" on the tomb, spin around three times, knock hard, and yell:

Marie Laveau, full of Voodoo. St. John is with thee. Bewitched art thou among women, and cursed is the solstice skull in your hand, the fiery Baptist. Hairdresser, whore-keeper, make magic for us sinners, now and before we drown in the bayou.

Amen.

Bushwick

Gentrification is not a glamorous word
    but it's what happened
or did you think this all came
    guilt-free?

This kitchen did not have
    a granite island before.
The coffee shop on
    the corner is new.
The skinny jean boutique
    came with them—
    them being me.

I am a gentrifier
    and I carry that guilt
    in my bones,
    but I will not move.
My college degree
    means I'm educated,
    not rich.

I never asked to be a pioneer.
I would never call myself a pioneer.
I am not here to uproot the delis

or the churches
or the liquor stores.
Stay planted on this earth
where you belong.

Give me empty warehouses,
give me abandoned storefronts,
but I am not here
to invade the spaces
neighborhood mainstays
and ancestors inhabit.

Join me, neighbors, in watching
the sunset melt into row houses.
I know you saw the red sun here first,
but can we face the sky together?

Saint Stephanie

Cat Power is blasting, but all I really hear is my friend Erica retching. She is bird-boned and high yellow by her own proclamation, yet her chiseled, golden cheeks are hidden in the depths of a PBR box. Though our classmates glance to her every now and then as she gradually fills the box with vomit, I am the only one watching Erica with rapt attention. I stand in the doorway, barely moving even after Big Mickey taps me on the back.

"Um, is she going to be okay?" he asks in the deep voice befitting of a large man, though not one as young as Big Mickey is.

"Yeah, she just has to get it all out," I say.

Big Mickey shrugs and leaves me in the doorway. Erica's head bobs up and down a couple more times before she pushes the box away and curls up on the floor. I sigh and walk over to pick up the box. Erica's eyes are closed, but the expression on her face is not a peaceful one. I head out the kitchen door and down the backstairs of the row house to the dumpster. Though the night is clear, my conscience is not.

I am an asshole. I know that now. But for all of college, I've been Saint Stephanie the Self-righteous, she who is angry and in denial. She the biracial girl who pals around with that other biracial one—the alcoholic, the bulimic, the clinically depressed—in part to commiserate far from the gaze of our white audience, in part to look better before them.

I never needed pills or booze to cope.

That fact, Saint Stephanie, does not make you better. You

may not be addicted to substances, but you are addicted to your inner rage.

I am not white.
I am not black.
I am not white.
I am not black.

It is a mantra and it is a curse.

The dumpster is, of course, no place for an epiphany, even with a million stars burning bright in the sky. So I dart back up the stairs, edge through the crowd in the kitchen, and scamper back to the living room. Erica is still on the floor. I crouch down to her so that our faces nearly touch. Mine is so much pinker than hers.

"Hey," I whisper. "We've got to get out of here."

Erica does not stir.

"Come on," I say as I rustle her. She grunts, but does not move. Even with her tiny frame, I know I cannot carry her. I signal to Big Mickey and he ambles over to us.

"Could you help bring Erica to my car? It's not because you're a guy or anything. You're just..."

"Much stronger than you?"

I roll my eyes and nod as I hug myself.

"Just don't hold her too close," I say. "She stinks."

Big Mickey scrunches his nose as he scoops Erica into his brawny chest. We then leave the house in silence and head down the block in search of my car. Despite being sober, I have no idea where I parked. All I know is that it had to be close because Erica had on heels and didn't want to stumble block after block in stilettos.

Once I locate my hunk of junk, I jiggle the key in the lock on the driver's side, shove a pile of books off the passenger seat, and open the passenger side door from the inside. Then I roll back into the driver's seat so Big Mickey can put Erica down. He buckles Erica's seatbelt and stands there, looking at me.

"Okay, well, thanks," I say.

"Yeah, no problem."

"See you in class on Monday," I add, feeling like I'm reading from a script.

"Stephanie."

"What?" I snap.

"I think Erica might need professional help," says Big Mickey. "Her drinking has gotten—"

"There's nothing we can do about that right now. Good night."

I roll up the windows with Big Mickey still standing there, glowing white in the moonlight. He is as white as my father and Erica's mother.

***

Erica lives on the first level of her building, so it's easy enough for me to drag her into her apartment. Her sprawling two-bedroom is always a dark, messy cavern, but tonight it exudes a menacing air.

"Hello?" I call out as I stand in the front door with Erica draped over my shoulder. When nobody answers, I bring Erica to the bathroom and seat her on the toilet.

I run to the kitchen to fetch cold water and splash it on Erica's face. She winces and perks up. Then I tip her head back and feed her water as if she were a baby sparrow I was nursing back to health.

"I'm tempted to put you to bed, but I'm afraid you won't wake up."

"And then you'll be the only mulatto in our class," Erica sputters. She paws the water cup out of her face as her chuckling grows into a giggle fit.

"Let's not forget that Shirley Plantation would lose their top slave re-enactor, too," I say slyly, poking fun at Erica's real-life college job.

"That's right," she laughs. "Can't let the plantation down."

"How about a cold bath?"

"For real?"

"Yeah, I know you have ice."

I bend over to turn on the faucet and turn around to find Erica making a failed attempt to remove her clothes. Her head is stuck in her blouse. I yank it off and help her wriggle out of her jeans, too. She kicked off her heels long ago.

"You're so good to me," Erica says as I hand her a towel.

"Don't say that."

"I don't mean you're perfect, but you *are* good to me."

I smile, though I don't say anything for the rest of the night. When we wake up, we are a bundle of limbs in the tub, pink and yellow entwined. All of the ice cubes have melted.

Altar to the Clam Ear

Instead of burying the body part
that brings me shame,
I will worship it
in a ceremony on the beach.
I will build an altar of
oyster shells and crab claws
and whisper incantations
in tune with the sea.
I will dance possessed.
I will light incense.
I will throw myself to and fro.
My deformed little ear
is a part of me,
and I will venerate it
with all my mermaid magic.

Saved

Your mother never belonged
at the Episcopal church.
Her brown face glowed even
without ongoing candlelight
and she never owned
a pastel cardigan in her life.

"Where is Virgin Mary?"
she whispered as you walked
down the nave to the pew
where your white husband sat.
Her dark head whirred like
Sinbad's golden owl as she
studied the stained glass and
sniffed the air for incense.

Every Christmas Eve,
your Harlem parish
blushed with poinsettias,
but you hated the Spanish
hymns and the weeping.
Even then, you embraced
self-loathing as your religion.

Any biracial child with
a white parent
stares down this choice:
to identify as the oppressed
or the oppressor.
You may be "brown and white"
in your rage-filled heart,
but the world rejects this answer.

You voice your choice every day
in what you eat, what you wear,
and who you love in the sweaty silence
of the night or jittering at the altar.

"There is no Mary here," you tell
your mother and slide in
next to your husband,
ever the guilty mutt.

Isaiah

Gabriela put the phone down and looked me in the face. She was my mother's age and, despite no relation, had my grandmother's hazel eyes, more green than chestnut. The magazine's cramped office meant that our desks were so close to each other that I almost ate my lunch in her lap every day.

"That was my friend," she finally said, stunned.

I nodded and continued typing my email to the priest/dentist I needed to interview for my article on Catholic service organizations in Central America.

Gabriela kept staring at me. I kept typing. Then I clicked 'send.' I turned back to her. Her mouth hung open, but no words came out.

"Which friend?"

"A friend at my old job. Our other friend gave birth four months into her pregnancy."

I straightened up as Gabriela sunk into her hands for a few moments and then rose again.

"The baby was born alive," she said. "But he was so small. He lived for fifteen minutes. They named him Isaiah. Then he died."

I sucked in my breath. "God."

"Fifteen minutes. And he died," Gabriela repeated as she fell back into her hands. "Why would God do that?"

I screwed up my face and lifted my palms.

Gabriela sighed. "My old co-workers want me to write the sympathy card."

I winced.

"I think this sort of thing affects us women most," she said.

Biting my lip, I nodded. Then I spent the rest of the afternoon refreshing my inbox and pretending to read the pope's new encyclical on the environment. Gabriela didn't touch her lunch.

When I got off work that evening, it was pouring. I ran out of the building and into the warm rain, splashing through the parking lot. My leather sandals almost slipped off. At the crackle of thunder, my heart skipped. I gulped and galloped toward my car.

I spent the fifteen-minute drive home gripping the steering wheel, trying to enjoy the summer hits on the radio. Somehow I pushed through seven inches of water and parked my car farther from my apartment than I would've liked. I gathered up my bags and tried running to the main door, but there was so much rain now that I tripped and lost my sandal to the flood gathering in the lot. Another crackle of thunder stopped me from chasing it. I hopped the rest of the way to the door.

When I reached the lobby, I shook myself dry and smiled a sad smile at the children playing by the front desk. My evening battle with the rain had lasted longer than Isaiah's whole life.

Deep in the Roots

Casper Rawlins never liked us playing in his fern-filled yard at the sleepy foot of Mill Mountain. But we chillun never liked him and we loved the sprawling magnolia on his lot. So we paid him no mind except to run away at the sight of his mean old self. He stood nearly seven feet tall like a bear on its hind legs, and his smile was fiercer than a possum's. Finn Jasper James, the redhead who lived on the other side of Casper Rawlins' house from me, said he saw him turn into a wolf once. Even the littlest of us knew that was far-fetched. Wolves hadn't roamed Virginia since the Civil War. Our granddaddies told us so.

No, Casper Rawlins was a witch doctor from New Orleans. He moved to Roanoke to wake up smelling the Blue Ridge air and face less competition in his wicked trade: ripping babies out of mamas who didn't want them and using them for his voodoo spells. He collected them in jam jars he yanked out from the garbage. I don't know who told the story first. All I know is that since I was old enough to leave my mama's yard and join the big kids in terrorizing the neighborhood, I took the tale as fact.

When I reached third grade, the big kids said Libby Messina, a high school junior who used to feed Mama's dogs when we visited Grandma in La Plata, ran around Big Lick kissing men. I never bore witness. What I saw was that Libby wore V-neck blouses, ruby lipstick, and gold rings on every finger. When I asked Finn how come she looked like a movie star, he said she looked like a hooker. And when I asked how come she kissed all those men, he said it was because she wanted to make babies.

"But she ain't grown," I replied, my teeny brow furrowed in

confusion. "Where she gonna put her baby at?"

"Her mama will probably hide her inside the house like how my Aunt Morgan did to my cousin Minnie."

"How come?"

He rolled his eyes and spat, "How can the big kids even stand you?" Then he hopped on his bike and sped off.

"You ain't a big kid, neither!" I shouted when he was too far away to hear me.

The summer after fourth grade ended, even I could tell Libby was pregnant. She didn't wear her elegant blouses anymore. All of her clothes had Virginia Tech and Hollins logos on them.

"My mama said all she gotta do is visit Casper Rawlins and he can take her baby away," said Finn one afternoon at our church playground. It was a Saturday and we were the only ones there trawling the jungle gym. We had started spending more time alone.

"Like that witch in Rapunzel?" I asked.

He shrugged. "I dunno. You know him and his spooky stuff. He's got a way."

Finn and I watched Casper Rawlins' house for days but never saw Libby near it. Then one day, Sarah Blackwell, a lanky sixth grader and notorious gossip, was walking by the playground when she spotted us.

"Guess what?" she called out as she headed toward where

we sat by the slide.

"What?" Finn said.

"My mama told me Libby went and had Casper Rawlins rip her baby out right good," she said, mischief flittering in her hazel eyes. "He paid her so he could use it for his voodoo magic."

"She still so big?" I asked.

"No, stupid," Sarah said. "He popped her like a bubble and now she's a string bean with boobies again."

Finn and I were silent. We heard a crow cawing overhead.

"Anyway," Sarah started again, suddenly solemn, "my mama's going to start praying for her. You should, too." Then she skipped off.

Finn and I stayed by the slide, where he held my hand until his mama called him in for supper.

The next day, I woke up with a red dot in my panties. Mama sighed and took me to the bathroom to show me how to use a sanitary napkin. As she washed the teeny stain out of my underwear, she got quiet and said, "I don't want you hanging around that Finn boy alone anymore. You understand?"

I nodded because, all of a sudden, I did.

The following summer, I had no friends. Finn had moved to Richmond and the girls in my grade had stopped noticing me. So I spent my days reading and spying on Casper Rawlins.

Two weeks after Independence Day, I was camped out in Mama's squash patch close to dark. Mama was still working and the house felt too big with me by myself. I squinted in the dim light, trying to finish the last pages of my book. That's when I heard the soft growl of a voice that belonged to one man and one man only:

"Heavenly Father, Your Love is eternal..."

Casper Rawlins was on his hands and knees before his magnolia, cupping a jar full of an off-white mass. Though I barely saw it, my frozen heart knew it was no turnip or herring. It was a baby receiving its Christian burial with Casper

Rawlins as the stand-in for a pastor. He cast no evil spell and looked smaller than I'd ever known. And now that I was a big kid, I had no eager ears to soak up my gossip, nobody to run to after the juicy sighting. Not that I had the courage to speak. For the rest of the summer, I was stricken with one question: When would it be my turn to feed Casper Rawlins' tree?

Biracial Shirley Temple

They say curly hair is pretty as long as
    it doesn't look too black—
        African, they mean.
        Savage, they think,
    because slaves are not beautiful,
    even if it was their great-granddaddies who
        did the enslaving
        and raping in the cotton fields,
            their white asses thrust in the sun.

Great-grandma had kink and frizz,
    but they swore *her* grandfather was a Spaniard.
To them, Berbers are not people of color
    because St. Augustine was a Berber
    and they cannot stomach an ounce of blackness.

Comb your hair straight, girl,
    so straight that the black in you
        scampers away
        in the night,
        swimming across the Potomac if it must.

Don't look too closely at the family album
    or you'll see Great-grandma
    was a Negro.

Jus Primae Noctis

You call this bed your splendor; I call it my cemetery.

This pillow is my tombstone. This sheet, death's veil.

Your prick has made a ghost of me, yet glaistig I am not. If I could sing, I might lure you and drink your blood, but voice have I none. No, Monseigneur, none.

As soon as my husband slipped the ring on my finger, you whisked me away to your dark, mossy castle. The fog filled my lungs and I fainted on your steed.

Open any book and you'll know how the story goes, 'The funeral follows the wedding.'

When the servant slumbering in the trundle bed bolts up at your bellowing, we shall have a witness to the death of my honor.

I had hoped the priest would deflower me instead. He is soft and white like a maggot, hardly fearful. But you are big, as big as a hairy highland coo, so fearful and yet still so soft, still so white.

I had hoped you would've been wearing chainmail— perhaps my silence would seem less pitiful. Perhaps my husband could forgive me then.

Do not call me 'Bonny' as I writhe beneath you. Bone the sorrowful lass and be done, bassa. Be done, be done, be done, be done, be done.

Teacher

No one ever believed I was half Mexican because I was milk white. People scanned me for just a hint of brownness, even the slightest swarthiness, and I had none. But I had my mother's moon-shaped face, broad mouth, and dusting of freckles on my nose and cheeks. Our eyelashes were equally long and thick, so much like a giraffe's, and our hands were near copies of each other. Still, everyone I encountered searched for the brown in me. They would've had to slice open my heart because that's where my brownness lived.

My mother was a 19-year-old college student when she barreled into El Paso on her 72-hour visa and never returned to Juárez. She fell in lust with an American, a Nordic man who, physically, was her opposite in every way. They holed themselves up in an Austin penthouse for a week. He said it was his deceased grandfather's property and that he was living there until his father sold it. They had take-out delivered to them three meals a day and stared out at the lake. Then one morning, my mother woke up to find herself alone. Her beau didn't leave so much as a note. Still, she waited for two days. When the knot in her stomach couldn't get any tighter, she packed her things and left. Her quest for adventure resulted in my birth and her fate cleaning houses for the next seventeen years.

I was six the first time I took up a sponge and dropped to my knees to scrub floors alongside my mother. We cleaned tangles of cat hair, drops of barbeque sauce, worlds of mold—whatever needed cleaning. We slept in the homes of white men who loved my mother, but their love was never requited. She didn't have the open heart of a teenager anymore. Whenever she broke up with them, we crashed at her childhood best friend's house. She and Alejandra would always spend that first night drinking tequila and singing rancheras.

Alejandra lived in a split-level in a planned community where peacocks roamed free. Born and raised in Guadalajara like my mother, Alejandra had achieved her version of the American dream by coming to Austin to work in a tech startup. Like my mother, she spoke with her hands, crushed hard on Vicente Fernández, and only ate guacamole made from scratch. Unlike my mother, she had all of her papers in order.

Somehow in all of this back and forth, I had never perfected my Spanish. I dribbled my vowels and slurred my 'r's instead of rolling them. My conjugations were never fully realized. I'd start with a verb and then mumble the ending, figuring I could make myself understood with enough emphatic gestures. Not that I ever needed to lean on my Spanish. I spoke English and Spanglish, the two official languages of Texas. As far as the average gringo Austinite was concerned, I was bilingual.

I knew this wasn't the life my mother had imagined and she was restless to get back to Mexico, but too ashamed to return to her upper-class parents and all the trappings of their high expectations. Besides, what life was there for me in Guadalajara? Still, her bouts of melancholy betrayed her. Even if I was a Texas girl through and through, my mother was not.

The night my life changed forever, I was a high school junior, cleaning a client's cowboy boot collection with my mother. There were snakeskin boots, turquoise boots, studded boots, even a red pair that glittered like Dorothy's slippers. We were on the floor of the client's walk-in closet and, for hours, neither one of us spoke. We simply brushed boot after boot after boot until we reached the very last pair.

"Silvia," my mother uttered at long last. She was trying to edge out a stubborn piece of dirt from the chestnut boot as she said it.

"Yeah?"

"I love you."

I dropped the boot I was holding. She hadn't said those words since I was tiny, before I even started school.

"I love you too," I said slowly as I picked up the boot, but continued staring at her. I always thought her hair was the prettiest I had ever seen—almost black, with an auburn sheen, and long, loose curls that hugged her shoulders. My own hair was ash blonde and thin, as fine as a baby's. I never liked it and in that moment, I liked it even less. My mother wore her hair down, per usual, and the flecks of auburn shone in the florescent closet light. She must've been the most glamorous boot cleaner there ever was.

We put the last pair of boots in their place on the shelf and gave the house a once-over before my mother checked a few boxes on the form in her binder. She tore off the bottom half and put it on the client's fridge. We loaded our bags into the car and went to Alejandra's house. The drive wasn't long, but it was long enough to let my thoughts wander. I noticed how black the sky was and wondered about all of the animals we didn't see in the night.

When I woke up, my mother was gone. I ran to the bathroom and scoured the rest of the basement, but she was nowhere in sight. It was a Saturday, so she would've rustled me awake so I could accompany her to a house or two before she dropped me off at the library to do homework.

"Mom!" I cried.

That's when I heard the pit-pat of Alejandra's feet on the basement steps.

"Good morning, Silvia," she said, smiling awkwardly. I realized we had never been alone together before then.

"Where's Mom?"

"Why don't you come upstairs and I'll tell you? I made breakfast."

I reluctantly followed her to the dining room table, where two plates of pancakes and a pitcher of orange juice awaited. I looked at Alejandra, then back at the meal, and then at Alejandra again.

"Sit down," she said.

I sat.

"Go ahead and eat," she said as she sat down.

"No. I need you to explain."

Alejandra cleared her throat. "Your mother has gone back to Guadalajara. She wants you to live me with me while you finish high school. Then she wants you to go to college. I have offered to help you apply for scholarships and cover some of your expenses."

I couldn't believe anything Alejandra was saying. I grabbed a fork and stabbed my stack of pancakes repeatedly.

"Silvia!"

"She didn't tell me anything!" I shouted. "She didn't even say good-bye!"

"Because she knew you would try to stop her."

"It's not too late."

"Yes, it is. She's been in Mexico for hours and should be arriving in Guadalajara soon."

"What's she going to do there?"

"Go to night school. Care for her parents. Live her life in the light, out of the shadows."

"What about me?"

"You can see her again when you finish college."

I must've glowered something fierce at Alejandra because she jumped back.

"She abandoned me and you're acting like it's nothing," I spat.

"It's not nothing. But it's going to be okay. We can begin going through college brochures tonight. One of my co-workers gave me his old ones. His daughter is a Longhorn now. She's studying—"

"I don't care!" I bellowed and pushed all of Alejandra's quaint breakfast set-up onto the floor. Pancakes went flying. Syrup splattered the walls. Berries rolled on the floor. Both of us ended up covered in powdered sugar and dissolved into tears on the floor.

When we recovered, Alejandra squeezed my small, kitten paw hands, so like my mother's. She wiped a patch of powdered sugar from my eyelid and said, "One day you'll understand what she did for you. Time is the greatest teacher."

I dropped into Alejandra's chest and waited for her to hug me. When she put her arms around me, she did so with all the tenderness I had longed for in my mother. We embraced until our arms grew weak and we felt compelled to wash the syrup out of our hair. I had homework to do. I had colleges to apply to. I had a life to live, even if I no longer shared it with my mother.

Richmond

I thought I missed you
    and then I remembered that you
    still have an entire avenue
    dedicated to Confederate generals,
    that a statue of Arthur Ashe
    was deemed unworthy
    of joining the Rebel line-up.
Those are the kind of Southern memories
    that sour even the sweetest tea.

Your Meteorite Dust

Did you marry a white man to protect you?

    To assert your whiteness?

    To melt into your brown arms

        and somehow make you lighter?

You are no alabaster beauty,

    but a beauty that gleams all your own

    as if a pearl met meteorite dust

    and rolled into half darkness,

    the lighter flecks still shining.

Your father was white.

What would Freud say about that?

    Would he blow the dust off your pearl?

Just remember—

once upon a time,

    you could not have married

        any man at all,

        thanks to Master.

Fruit On Top of Her Head

The few times I stood
face to face with
my white grandfather,
he told me that
my brown mother
looked like Carmen Miranda.
His blue eyes lit up
as brightly as Times Square
and he squeezed
my yellow hand
as he said it.
I always replied,
"But Mommy doesn't
have fruit
on top of her head."

Today, I would reply
that Carmen Miranda is
Brazilian
and my mother is
Salvadoran
and that they only
resemble each other
in that neither one is blonde.

"So maybe you can stop
exoticizing them now, Grandpa."

Last Rites

Midnight Mass meant incense while les réveillons meant feasting. We, the bundled and the hungry, greedy for buche de Noel, darted from the cathedral to our tiny house by the dormant rose garden. The stars were bright that night and bigger than we would ever be.

I stomped and clapped the whole way up the hill, marveling that I could see my breath while there were palm trees in Bethlehem.

When the five of us huddled by the fireplace, you took us under your wings. Papa poured himself a drink. Dinner would wait.

All month, you had seen a flurry of medical folks. Each visit proved dimmer, darker, blacker than the last. You'd been met with grim faces, whispers, tears. The diagnosis was dour for your cancerous womb. You'd live to welcome the New Year, but not 'til spring.

But, you said, Christmas cheer should not die so soon. We had a goose in the oven and cake to spare, a real tree and merry Nativity scene, and five hearts beating boldly.

When Papa joined us by the fireplace, we held hands, as we would the following year, singing, "Sleep in heavenly peace," until the words vanished from our throats.

The Hoarder's Daughter

As the designated driver, you are the no-fun queen of judgment rolling through the McDonald's drive-thru at 3 a.m. on a Saturday. A classmate you hate—the know-it-all mansplainer who shares two of your classes—pays for everyone's burgers and fries. With the car full of drunk, hungry people, his generosity means something. But you still can't stand him, so you take advantage by ordering extra food. Two of everything your heart desires. Maybe leftovers for tomorrow? Maybe the rest of the week?

You are, after all, a college student with no campus meal plan. You, the scholarship kid, cannot afford to turn down free food. OK, it's not totally free. Who could forget that you're driving the goddamn car? It's the kind of autonomy you could not have imagined five years ago—being out in the middle of the night, driving, socializing. Five years ago, you were burdened with stuff—literal, physical stuff.

You were buried in your mother's ever-growing collections, suffocated by her love of red-headed porcelain dolls because people were always throwing out the ginger ones; kitchen utensils, big and small and rusty and non-matching; Laura Ashley dresses in four sizes too small, no matter that they look like sofa covers; mildewed books about Ireland because everyone keeps the good ones on their coffee table forever so they can always talk about their great-great-great-great-grandfather and the Potato Famine with company when other topics of conversation run dry.

Your father never said anything except that your mother grew up poor and that you were lucky to never taste poverty. But you can't invite friends to a house like that.

You can't find a private nook in a house like that because you can't breathe in a house like that. You can only exist in a house like that, and your mother insisted that you spend all of your time there. You, her only and most precious child, were part of her collection. When you weren't at school, you were practically sitting on one of her shelves, just like one of her porcelain dolls.

College was the only way to get out. The day your college acceptance letter arrived, you dug through piles to fish out the few objects of any value to you and packed your suitcase. Then you gazed mournfully at that suitcase all summer long until August when you could finally escape. Somehow, you won a full scholarship without ever mentioning you were a virtually homebound hoarder's daughter.

The burgers and fries come out at a glacial pace, so by the time the brown paper bags fill up the car, you step on it and zip over to the river. You're going to eat with a view. Maybe the boy you hate will stop prattling on about how he could be the next Steven Spielberg.

When you get there, you roll down the windows and inhale the smell of the wet earth. You and your drunk classmates stare at the moonlight hitting the water, the stars cartwheeling in the sky, silhouettes of government and corporate buildings that remind you that there's more to this place than your university. Your little city is bigger and more glamorous at night. For you, in this moment, it is the perfect size.

"Okay, Truth or Dare," slurs a girl who sometimes copies your Spanish homework. It's completely out of nowhere. Even the boy you hate has been silent for a spell. All of you were so mesmerized by the current.

"I'm too lazy to do anything," says a girl from your study group.

"Then you can choose Truth every time," scoffs the Spanish copier. "Like, it's not exactly a new strategy."

"Everyone in this car is totally done except for Aileen," says the study group girl. "Let's go home."

"No. Just one round. We haven't played a game all night."

"Who cares? Let's go to bed."

The boy you hate remains silent as the two girls go back and forth. You also stay quiet. As you look to the boy, your mind jumps to the time he served up a heaping portion of *Well, actuallys* during a class discussion on women's suffrage. If it weren't for his wallet, he wouldn't even be in your car.

"Fine! Truth!" shouts the study group girl.

"It's about freakin' time," says the Spanish copier. "Have you ever peed during sex?"

"Yeah. I've run up to go to the bathroom once or twice."

"No, like, have you peed during intercourse?"

"Ew! No!"

"Promise?"

"Yeah. Promise."

"Whatever. I don't believe you."

"Well, it's the truth. This is Truth or Dare. I wouldn't lie."

"Okay," the Spanish copier sighs. She crosses her arms and nods at the study group girl. "Now, you have to ask Boy Toy over here."

Even though it's study group girl's turn to talk, all of us are looking at the boy you hate. He is tense and small in the yellow cast of the streetlamp by our parking spot. His nose twitches.

"Truth or dare?"

"Truth."

"Aw, man!" the Spanish copier groans and hits the window.

"Hey, watch it," you say.

"Whatever, this car looks like it came from a salvage lot," the Spanish copier mumbles.

"You don't like it, you can walk home," you say. Then you face the boy you hate. "So, Truth?"

"Yeah, truth," he says.

"What's your biggest secret?" asks the study group girl.

The boy you hate clears his throat. "My mom's a hoarder."

Your stomach drops.

"No way!" the Spanish copier gasps. "As bad as in that TV show?"

"Yeah," he says, much lower than before. "My parents'

house caught on fire last year because of the mess. My mom was cooking and somehow something caught fire and soon the whole house was in flames because she had all these piles of newspaper everywhere. It was all over the local news. They showed my parents' mess and everything. The town issued a safety memo about the hazards of hoarding and how it can cause fires and obstruct passageways for firefighters."

You envision your own childhood home in flames. The porcelain dolls' hair catches on fire, their faces melt, their dresses become ashes.

"But your parents are alive?" the Spanish copier asks.

"Yeah, and they're in a new house now. Their insurance company paid for it. It's still embarrassing, though. Everybody in town knows. Before that, it was a secret. We never had anybody over."

Nobody responds and you feel yourself getting hot. You grip the wheel very tightly, so tightly, it hurts, and blurt, "I'm exhausted. Let's go."

"Not yet!" the Spanish copier pouts. "You and me haven't gone yet."

"Who cares? I'm driving and I say it's time to go home, so we're going. I have to write my research paper tomorrow."

"Ugh, you're so boring. It's just our first drafts that are due, anyway. Who even cares? It's, like, A for effort until the final thing is due."

"Well, I want to get the real work out of the way. Then when

I go to write the final—"

"Okay, okay! Nobody cares! Let's go."

You glare at the Spanish copier. When you glance at the other two, you realize they are falling asleep. You start up the car, admire the river for a second, and head up the road, toward the first apartment. It belongs to the boy you hate—a boy you now hate a little less.

Carry This Weight

I carry this mattress from Butler Library to Philosophy Hall, but it's not my heaviest burden. Though it has no history of bedbugs—I zip this sucker tight—it has a history of rape. Don't like that word? Neither does the university president. Nobody does.

Nobody likes getting raped, either. Nobody likes being pushed against a wall, having their legs forced and folded into a biology class froggy tuck, and then getting rammed in the ass, without any lube and without their consent.

Pardon me if I'm stating the obvious. Apparently, to some, it's not so obvious. My job is to help them see it. They won't see the sip of gin I took that night. They won't see what started out as something fun and devolved into inspiration for my reoccurring nightmare. They sure as hell won't see me getting anally raped. But every day, they can see where I got raped.

This is the ugly memento riding my back. This evidence comes with me to class, to the dining hall, and back to the dorm. It may be my performance art. It may be my thesis. But first, it was my life. It was always truth, never fiction, never art for art's sake, and never just for the grade.

For as long as we are both on campus, I will carry this weight. He made this bed, but I have to sleep in it.

Father-Daughter Mirror Play

The gleaming mirror in our Harlem rental
reminds me that times are good
because we own something clean.
It reflects my image more luminously
than my image has ever
been reflected before.
Now that I am bleeding once a month,
that matters to me.
Now that I can smell the stink that
comes with forsaking deodorant for a day,
that matters to me.
I long for the kind of hair
girls have in magazines, but that is not my hair.
It is the straight and flaxen hair of my father.

When Daddy and I stand side by side
and stare at the mirror, I want to see our souls.
Instead, I focus on how my yellow skin
contrasts to his ivory complexion
My wiry curls grow out, not down.
My nose is broad. My lips are broad.

"But our eyes crinkle exactly the same way
when we laugh," he says.

And when we laugh, they do.

Loving v. Virginia

Veiled in the night.
    Wed beneath the moon.
        The stars bear witness to vows
            uttered by a white man & a black woman
            or a white woman & a black man.
                This love can only live in shadows.

A moment of silence for the salt & pepper that touched on the table.

[...]

Half a century ago,
        the ebony & ivory couple feared the sun
            because neighbors feared them,
            because neighbors feared the rise of mutts and mutants,
            because neighbors feared what this love said about their hate:
                hatred in heaps & heaps like hay after the harvest.

Fingers laced,
        legs entwined,
            a crisscross of complexions.

A curly-haired child born in the brush,
        scratched by twigs & dry leaves,

the mulatto still cries.
The mulatto still bleeds.

The human heart is one color
    and human souls are every color at once.
        These the consistent color schemes that bond us.
            Only bodies break this rule of nature:
                bodies of every hue,
                    bodies of every shade.

Love renders us beautiful,
            even when we are insatiable,
but the man who is not my president is insatiable,
            not beautiful,
    Love, the only purity on earth,
            racial purity, a falsehood.
                Bleed, mulatto. Bleed.
                    Your blood, the same color as Trump's blood
                    your heart, the same color as Trump's heart.

School Days

Even though the yellow bus wheeled around before Mama rose, I always kissed her good-bye before I left because when I returned, she would not be mine to kiss.

I sat silently on that bus for eons, staring at my toes, while the others shouted, "Your mama's the best!"

They meant the best at banging. The best at head and hand jobs, at kneeling and choking, at fisting and catching.

For the next eight hours, I escaped through books, my refuge from their spit, my refuge from their looks, my refuge from Mama and her kinky antics, my refuge from her men and sexual semantics.

But when the yellow bus wheeled around again, I shook like a sapling tormented by the rain.

Because I knew the front door would be open. Because I knew there'd be empty liquor bottles. There'd be the sounds of wild animals in pain.

Sometimes, there were not just sounds, but sights— like Mama bent over the kitchen counter, huffing as a man came rushing at her from behind. His groin slapped her tail and he pulled her mane. She neighed and whinnied, whimpered and whined. And I couldn't ever do my homework there again.

So sometimes I skipped the yellow bus and crept to the school library where I studied and slept. There'd be no yellow bus the next morning.

And I could pretend I had no mama, only books.

Big Fish

The stench of roach spray
clouded the apartment
the day my
college acceptance letter
arrived.

I had netted a whale,
a full-tuition scholarship.
I felt victorious
yet confused.

Had the sea been too shallow?
Had the whale been too weak?

Perhaps I was no
skilled fisherman after all.

"Affirmative action"
was the rumor that
stank up the high school hallways,
more pungent than roach spray.

I sat on the beach
and sulked in the sand.

I cut my toe on a razor clam,
but my heart hurt too much
for me to cry over physical pain.

The sharks could probably
smell my blood from
their home among the waves.
But I had other concerns
as I scanned the horizon:
Is there a ship meant just for me?

Clam Ear

I was not born a mermaid,
but that is the tale I told myself
beginning in childhood.
    {We weave origin stories
        to survive.}
How else to explain my
    little crushed clam ear?
    How it looks more mollusk-like than human-like
    the way it curls in all the wrong places,
        a catastrophe of design?
If there were no photographs or illustrations
    depicting my deformity
    in any book I ever encountered,
        surely there was a reason:
        I must be a mythical creature,
        meaning my deformity was
            not a deformity,
            but magic.
Welcome to the lushness of a kindergartener's rationale,
    more so imagination at work than true logic
        {We fall into the world of imagination
        to survive.}
Instead of walking the school hallways,
    I saw myself navigating a coral reef,

a place as vibrant as my young mind.
The bright hues embraced me
from chartreuse to indigo.
The sea smell seduced me
in salty swirls.
The swishing of fish and plants
enchanted both of my ears,
the beautiful one
and
the crushed one,
sea sounds in my mermaid ear.
{We indulge our senses
to survive.}

Copied

When you died, I made copies of your portrait. It was 3 a.m. at the 24-hour copy shop and I smelled like someone had dumped an entire bottle of Burt's Bees bubble bath on me because that's exactly what I did to myself when you popped out from between my legs. You were a jellybean. You were so pink, I could've eaten you. Placed you on my tongue and savored you. To bring you into my body again. Make us two beings in one again. Then we would've been Mommy and baby, splashing in the tub. Dream Daddy might've swooped in with a rubber ducky or toy ship. The perfect scrapbook moment.

Instead, the olive-green sweats from my fat days were barely staying on my hips and my huge Hanes Her Ways were bunched up to my belly button. Maybe I had lost weight too quickly, I nagged myself, tugging at my baggy T-shirt with "Save the Ta-tas" printed across the front. I had on no makeup. I had on no bra. All I had on was a base layer of grief and an overcoat of nostalgia. The one cashier on duty pretended not to stare when I hobbled over to the copier. Since there were no other customers, I took center stage. Gaze upon my sadness, boy. Gaze upon this once-upon-a-time mother and her hands turned raisins from four hours spent in the tub.

When I nodded at the cashier, he nodded back. He was sallow and heavy-lidded. Otherwise, he might as well have been a cardboard cutout behind the counter. I didn't register any of his other features. Instead, I wanted to imagine yours.

I had always hoped that you—or whichever baby came along— would have my mother's dimples and almond eyes.

Your father wasn't a particularly handsome man, but still, I wanted you to have his height, his freckles, and the laugh I once heard daily. Most of all, when I looked at you, I wanted to know that you were mine. I didn't want there to be a mistake at the hospital. I didn't want you to spend eighteen years in someone else's home. If you made the front page of the newspaper, it would be for an award or a good deed, not some scandal.

All those musings were old, of course—three decades in the making, renewed this evening. When Lionel Richie blared on the radio, he reminded me that you were gone. The real scandal was that your death would never make the newspaper. You would never win an award or perform a deed of any kind. No one would ever take your headshot or your mugshot. You had had no hair, no lips, no chin, no distinguishing features at all. If you resembled your grandmother at all, then you resembled her prenatally.

If.

I had no photos to compare. You were a two-centimeter chunk of raw chicken breast drenched in blood. Something tells me your great-grandmother—a woman who only hung paintings of flowers on her walls—wouldn't take or keep such photos, even if she could. When Grandma was conceived, the ultrasound hadn't even been invented yet.

But in the sonogram, there was no blood. You were black and white, which meant that I could fill in the colors. I could choose your dreams. I could paint the life that would have been.

I stood back and watched the paper shoot out of the

machine, sheet by sheet by sheet. Through the copier's beeps, I asked God why your father had gone out of town this weekend. Even though this was a man I now knew mainly through the PowerPoint printouts he left on the breakfast counter; his presence would've meant not losing you alone.

The past couple of years, he had hustled for promotion after promotion so we could ready our nest for you. We made love in between presentations and meetings and deadlines. In those 26 months we tried for you, we watched Britcoms and held hands until I finally gave in and rolled over. Now I had to tell him that instead of rolling over all those times, we should've just watched another episode of Fawlty Towers. We barely discussed the weather—except when it might change his commute or delay a business trip.

Maybe I would call him in the morning. Maybe I would just wait until he came home. Maybe I'd mutter something during the credits of Are You Being Served? These days, I no longer rolled over. One TV show after dinner was never enough and conversation was too much.

When the copier spat out the last image of you, I pressed three hundred printouts to my chest. The cashier nodded as I walked out. Then I headed to the car in a daze.

Once home, I went straight for the kitchen drawer and grabbed two rolls of tape. I inched toward the nursery because it scared me. Yet when I got to the doorway, all of the teddy bears comforted me. I sat down in the rocking chair with a green bear motif. Another one with blue bears faced the window. One for me, one for Daddy or Grandma. I rolled two tape doughnuts for the first sheet of paper and then stuck you on the wall. I repeated the action three hundred times. You replaced the teddy bear wallpaper.

Dark as it was, the room became a womb. I was inside of you, just as you had been inside of me. I would sleep and maybe when I woke up, you would be born, and your father would be somewhere in the stars. Genesis with no Adam. We would be blind for four days until we saw the sun. Then life would really begin. But we'd have to be quiet and wait for our Eden.

These Are Not the Stories

These are not the stories
your mother tells you
growing up.

Tuabuelo eraunindio.
Tuabuelo era unesclavo.

Otherwise,
you may never
beam the way children
are meant to beam
and blossom the way
children are meant
to blossom.

Era un hombre enojado.
Era un hombre sujeto a pasiones.

Because they are the stories
that make a child wilt
and dry out in the sun
instead of uniting
them *with* the sun,
a glowing face

of possibility,
of memories
full of blue skies.

Y poreso me pegaba.
Y poreso me violaba.

You can only hear
these stories
once you've
hardened
from pebble
to boulder.

The Theatre Department

When you study acting as a biracial girl in the South,
    you will never portray Scarlett O'Hara,
    only ever Mammy
    because your program head does not think "protagonist"
    when she sees a mulatto.
You are an accessory, like the dogwoods that dot a plantation.

Bleaching cream is not expensive becomes your chant
    as you wait in line at the drugstore
    on a July night when your high yellow complexion
    browns below the florescent lights.

"It's all in your head, your nappy, nappy head," says Mom
    as she ruffles your black curly hair,
    but she's whiter than you even thought God made white
    because she's whiter than bleached possum bones.
This woman is your mother, not for her skin, but for her blood.

That is, the blood of the Scotch-Irish who defeated the British
    and wrestled wolves and brown bears out of Appalachia,
    while your father's people battled bolls in the cotton fields,
    rising up to overseers when picking cut up their hands and souls.

You read scripts and fall in love with characters not written for you,

only it takes you two and a half years to realize it.

Then you lock eyes with a needle

and, after one night of passion with a sewing machine,

decide to design costumes.

Costumes are an icon, you tell yourself, because everyone remembers

what Liz Taylor wore in *Cleopatra*

and how Dorothy dressed in *The Wizard of Oz*.

They remember and they don't mind whose fingers do the work.

Porcelain fingers, mahogany fingers, or high yellow fingers.

This was the role written for me, the half-breed in the back.

My Mother, the Nanny

After school came the march of the mommies and nannies.
They crowded the hallways and the lawn by the bus lanes,
waving permission slips and jackets and sports equipment.

An imaginary line divided the white women from the brown ones—
the women volunteering to be there from the ones paid to be there.

Except my mother never stood with the other mothers.
She joked and confided and gossiped with the nannies,
who were women who also hailed from faraway lands
and dreamt dreams in a language other than English.

"Is that your nanny?" mothers and classmates would ask,
sometimes even in the presence of my mother,
as if she could not understand what they said.
And when I said she was my mother,
they almost always replied that
we looked nothing alike.

They could only see brown and white.

Dirty, Dusty Beans

You scraped the beans off the floor
and said, "Don't be so clumsy."

Because our fridge was empty,
our EBT card was empty.
Our stomachs were empty.

"We can't afford to
feed the roaches."
So I ate that spoonful
of dirty, dusty beans.

Then I headed to St. James
for a sack of cans:
canned herring,
canned liver,
canned beets,
canned bread,
canned okra—
all foods designed for the poor.

But I didn't head straight home.
I headed to the club
and signed up

for an audition.

"Do you need a resume?"
I asked.
The manager laughed,
flashing her gold teeth.
"What? You got a PhD?"
"Actually, I do."
She froze.

"This pays more
than adjuncting," I said.
She nodded.
"As long as you can dance."

I can dance as long
as it means no more
dirty, dusty beans.

"Yeah, I can dance."
And I flexed my calves.

My Non-existence Under a Trump Administration

When my mother patted the black tufts of hair on my head and gazed into my dark eyes for the first time, she was not a U.S. citizen. But, in my newborn pinkness, I was. The year was 1988 and it was an unseasonably warm day in November less than one week after Halloween. I was experiencing the world outside of my mother's womb in healthy, even breaths that would not have been possible had it not been for my mother's emergency C-section. With my umbilical cord wound around my neck, my birth was almost my undoing. My tiny mother was exhausted, but relieved to welcome all eight pounds of me—alive!—with my American father by her side.

The site of this initial meet and greet was a regional hospital on a long, winding road in my hometown of Arlington, Virginia. As part of the Washington, D.C. metro area, the pipsqueak county may be one of the smallest in the United States, but it has one of the largest Salvadoran populations in the country. This is worth mentioning because my mother is Salvadoran. She, like the majority of her fellow Salvadoran immigrants, came to the United States to escape her homeland's civil war.

When my parents met and fell in love in El Salvador, starting a family there was not a consideration. My father's broadcast career was based in the United States and the El Salvador my mother knew as a child was quickly disappearing. No parent dreams of raising their children among ricocheting bullets and bloodshed. But my father didn't want just any wife; he wanted my mother, and he was willing to wait for the notoriously sluggish U.S. Citizenship and Immigration Services as they hemmed and hawed. Eventually, they gave Leticia Cristina Sanchez Gomez a stamp of approval and she bid El Salvador farewell forever.

As soon as my mother's papers were approved, my parents started their life together not far from Miami's sparkling beaches. They were married at St. Bernard de Clairvaux Church, a 12th-century Spanish monastery that had also witnessed a great migration. Newspaper mogul William Randolph Hearst purchased the ancient structure in the 1920s and had it disassembled stone by stone so it could be shipped from Spain to the United States. But like my mother, the monastery—which filled an astounding 11,000 wooden crates—experienced a period of limbo.

After the monastery arrived in New York, Hearst couldn't afford to have it reconstructed. Thus the stones sat in a Brooklyn warehouse for more than a quarter of a century. It wasn't until Hearst passed that hope for the monastery was reignited. Two entrepreneurs bought the grand edifice from the Hearst estate and gave it a second life in Florida. They paid the modern equivalent of $20 million for the privilege of putting together what a 1953 issue of *Time Magazine* dubbed "the biggest jigsaw puzzle in history."

Unlike the monastery, my parents did not reach the end of their journey in Miami. Two years after their wedding, they moved to Washington when my father accepted a job there. That was how my mother found herself moving from the capital of El Salvador to "the capital of Latin America" (as Miami has been nicknamed) to the capital of the United States. El Salvador's civil war certainly played a role, but my mother ultimately moved out of love and stayed out of love.

But, today, my parents' story would be even less likely

than it was thirty years ago. U.S. borders have gotten tighter and tighter and Central Americans fight for green cards. Even children in some of El Salvador's most violent regions have trouble seeking refuge in the United States. I'll never forget covering a Catholic Charities meeting for parents who wanted more information about the USCIS Central American Minor Program. Under this competitive program, Central American parents who live in the U.S. but who have children living in Central America can petition to have their children join them. One of the women fled the room crying when she learned that her child had aged out of the requirements. Even though the Catholic Charities chapter had been assisting parents with paperwork for months, the coordinator told me not a single child had been approved to come to the U.S.

President-elect Donald Trump says he wants to deport all 11 million estimated undocumented people now living in the U.S. He says he wants to strengthen U.S. borders and build a wall between here and Mexico. He has accused Latinos of being criminals, of stealing Americans' jobs, of tearing their own families apart through immigration.

Any time Trump rages against Latinos and immigrants, I think of my parents and how they would not be together if he had been president during their courtship. My parents never would've married in that Spanish monastery. My mother never would've wailed in that Arlington hospital. My father never would've worried that his daughter would die before he met her. And me? I never would've been born.

Loving the White in Me

Did you grow up with Spanish at home?

It's the first question most people ask
    when they learn my mother is from El Salvador.

White people want to know how brown I am.
Brown people want to know how white I am
    because The Donald is threatening to build a wall,

How outraged will I be when Trump grabs
    an intern's pussy in the White House?

How sickened will I be when Trump folds
    his daughter over his presidential desk?

Will I be as furious when he deports 11 million people
    as when he assaults a white woman?

I am trying to love the white in me every single day
    because I fought so hard to love the brown.

We mutts are half oppressor,
    half oppressed.

Women like my father's mother—
        blonde,
        blue-eyed,
        so-called Christian—
voted for Trump.

But not my grandmother.
She wanted Bernie,
        so she voted for Hillary.

It's women like her who remind me
        that I don't have to bury my whiteness
        as I plan to bury Trump
                deep
                deep
                deep in the darkest holes of my heart
                for him to grow blinder and blinder,
                like an orange newt with shrinking eyes
        while the rest of America dances outside
        beneath a sun that shines only for justice.
                Even the white ones dance.

Richmond Ennui

You used to scour the rag shops in Southside,
     where black families lived in trailers
     and row houses that were termite fodder.
Then you would realize costumes for white actors
     and white audiences in the white parts of town.

Southside reminded you of where your father grew up
     in Roanoke before the speculators descended
     upon Star City and razed down the rickety
     home where six generations of freemen lived.

There, Nana made the best collards in the Commonwealth—
     until you went vegan and wouldn't touch them
     for fear of bacon.

"Fear that white mama of yours," spat Nana
     when you first pushed the bowl of greens across the table.
"Fear them white politicians in your uppity ole Richmond."
"I'm tired of them, too, Nana. I'm tired of everything there."

You pictured the black neighborhoods and their sagging schools.

"You think I ain't tired? You gotta stop before you fade."
"I don't know how I can stop being tired when everything's so tiring."

Nana sucked her teeth and thus ended the last conversation
you had with her before she perished in her nursing home.

You pricked your fingers with a thousand needles that semester
and you still had one more year to survive,
so, naturally, you became the mulatto in mourning.

"Lavinia's not really black," said a classmate one rehearsal night.
"She acts so white. She's a really cool girl, not ghetto."
You tightened your jaw as you ripped out a seam
for the blonde, svelte lead in the play.
Nobody saw you hunched in the dark corner.

Later, as you fitted the lead's costume,
you said, "You look like my mother,"
and her glacier blue eyes flashed in horror.

Twelve. More. Months.

Cursed by a Sea Witch

In my mermaid life,
I could have been born with
    two perfectly shaped ears,
        round and smooth,
        barnacle-free,
        ideal for holding my seaweed-length locks
        out of my dewy face
        as I zipped in and out of coral caves.
But I was not born formed as other mermaids are.
I shot out of my mother and into the ocean
    with a clam ear,
        a defect I buried under my heaps of hair.
Who in Neptune's kingdom defined perfection
    and neglected to include me?
Who touched my mother's womb and
    destined me to swim the seas
    just short of perfection?
I blame the corpulent sea witch
    who dwelled among the eels,
        feasting on lowlier creatures
        to strengthen her evil powers.
She cursed me with an ugly ear
    and she cursed me with the shame
        I carried for it.

The shame is worse than
    the deformity itself.
The shame is a sea slug,
    buried so deep in the mud
    that it only sees darkness.
The shame is a crab
    left to die in the boiling sun,
    agonizing for hours on the hot sand.
The shame is...
    The shame just is.

A Recipe for Speculators

1. Buy a house

> in a neighborhood with no trees

> or streetlamps

> or hope

> or prosperity

> because the city has forgotten

> its people

> and their dreams,

>> at least these people,

>> at least these dreams.

2. Renovate the house

> beyond recognition.

> Remove all of its character

>> for a uniform catalog look

>> that could pass for anywhere.

3. Flip the house

> by luring yuppies

> to a branded "new frontier"

>> because they want to be pioneers.

4. Repeat

> until your city could be any city

> in America.

A McMansion in Fredericksburg

Your diploma hangs on the wall and you are homebound,
　　　　one hour from Richmond, one hour from Washington, D.C.
Most days, you do not leave your room,
　　　　that temple to theatre, that temple to cinema.
　　　　You have amassed your relics:
　　　　　　　　Criterion DVDs and thrift shop photographs,
　　　　　　　　costumes you designed and others you stole,
　　　　　　　　books on the history and theory of design,
　　　　　　　　graded papers and sketches and playbills.

Cat Power reminds you that once you wanted to be the greatest.
You play the record because, yes, you have a record player—
　　　　another reminder of art school, of life from months ago.

Your father is one of those rare black men who white men call "sir,"
　　　　and that is why you live in a McMansion in Fredericksburg,
　　　　where a creek trickles among honeysuckle in your backyard.
Sometimes your mother sits in the parlor staring at the creek
　　　　while she shines her Daughters of the American Revolution pin.
　　　　You wonder what ghosts she sees.

"What will you do today, Lavinia?" she asks
　　　　when you emerge from your room for the first time that day.
　　　　It's 4 o'clock.

"Apply for jobs, I guess," you say with a shrug.
    But you've applied and applied and applied
    and nobody has called.
You think back to high school when all the boys wanted to date blondes.
    You, kinky-haired one, were never blonde.
Yet employers are not the same as teenage boys, says your rational side.
Eventually your existence will not consist of watching Cary Grant films
    and eating chips and candy in bed.

"You're just in a rut," your mother tells you as she studies the creek.
    Not making eye contact has become natural between you—
    you almost forget not all daughters resent their white mothers.
You almost scream, "Why are you so beautiful?"
    Instead you ask, "Why did you never have a job?"
    "I married young" is the simple response.
You wish you had married young, but nobody ever asked.
"Besides, I never went to college."

You are too imaginative for this vinyl palace by the creek.
Too dark, too kinky-haired, too other.
You never asked to be a mulatto princess.

The Lucky Ones

Before Tinder and Grinder and OKCupid, we had the East End Bridge. It was not a land of love but a land of fucks and you could give as many, or as few, as you wanted. But you came there to lie in a bed of used condoms, shit-covered leaves, and broken glass with one intention: to give, or receive, at least one fuck. Alcohol and drugs were merely appetizers, and the only restaurant you go to just for appetizers is TGI Fridays. All others either win or lose you with the main course.

Summer after summer, the East End Bridge boasted a loyal customer base. Even in the wintertime, you could find local kids embracing one another, panting little clouds of their warm breath into the air, stretched out on a strip of cardboard if they were lucky. A mediocre meal is better than no meal at all. Everybody's got to eat. Or as my mom used to say, "Everybody's got needs."

We went there because most of us didn't have our own bedrooms like kids in the movies. Most of our parents didn't have jobs, at least not steady ones, which meant our trailers were almost never conveniently absent after school, and none of us had our own cars, let alone hot rides with leather seats. Privacy was another middle class luxury we couldn't afford. You either went all the way under the East End Bridge or saved yourself for marriage like Pastor Jenkins commanded from the pulpit of our otherwise-abandoned strip mall church. *Chastity is a virtue. Chastity is divine. Chastity will save you from hellfire.*

I had planned on saving myself for marriage less out of a concern for hell than a concern for cutting myself on a smashed bourbon bottle under the East End Bridge. It was no bed of roses, even that time our biology teacher,

Ms. Russell, discarded fifteen bouquets there. Her fiancé sent the flowers, one for each month they had dated, after she found him cheating with his niece. A few of us were huddled around a bonfire one Saturday night when it started raining petals and thorns. While the blanket of red and green improved the scenery a little, our spot under the bridge was still as sorry as it had ever been. Yes, I'd claw myself out of town if I had to and lose my virginity some place clean and quiet, anywhere but there. I didn't think that was too much to ask.

Then I saw Pastor Jenkins fucking my mom doggy-style.

Most kids hear their parents having sex at some point, but few have the misfortune of catching them in the act. Best case scenario, it's Mom and Dad tossing and turning under the sheets with a moan here and there. His cock and her snatch remain a mystery. Worst case scenario, it's Mom with someone old enough to be your grandpa, both of them playing it rough with every wrinkle and sweat gland in plain sight. Her tits are flopping faster than your cousin flips hash browns at the Waffle House down the street, his ass looks like something that belongs on a 100-year-old toad, and both parties are breathing so hard, you're convinced they're about to break. It's poignant when the ancient pastor cries, "Jesus!"

I yelled, "I hate you," as he withdrew from Mom and ran out the door. I escaped so quickly that I never saw them register that I had witnessed the debacle. After that, I thought nothing of "fornicating" under the East End Bridge.

His name was Ned, he was in my Spanish class, and he rode me on a flattened Budweiser box.

Central Virginia Office Parks

At last, a job.

    You emerge from your parents' McMansion in the woods.

Ann Taylor will do—slacks with creases,

a blouse with too many buttons.

    This is adulthood.

    This is why you went to college.

    Now you have a salary, a briefcase.

You may not have the respectability of whiteness,

    but you have the respectability of a 9-to-5.

Even as a mulatto,

    you are the darkest person in the office park.

    This is Central Virginia.

    There are black people in Central Virginia.

    They are the descendants of people who built

        the plantations

        and presidents' homes.

    Your father is one of them.

    So where are they?

One day you have to deliver a package to another office

and you see a black man wiping down the tables and desks.

    He is the janitor.

They never taught you how to use spreadsheets in theatre school.

Once as an undergrad,

    you made a Powerpoint on the history of costume design.

Here, you make a Powerpoint every week.

You never touch a sewing machine.

You never use your hands at all,

    except to click and clack at the keyboard.

You thought theatre would be the last den of whiteness you inhabited.

You thought that you were made to use your nimble fingers.

"Punch in the clock. Collect your paycheck. Learn some discipline."

These words become your mother's constant refrain.

You never remind her that not a single generation of women

    in her family worked outside the home

    and that she has always had a housekeeper.

She never learned how to grow the tobacco

    or harvest the Christmas trees

    that made her great-granddaddy rich.

How many times a day can you listen to an office copier whir

    before you go insane?

You, the Immigrant's Daughter

I parted your lips and lapped at you like a kitten laps milk, but you couldn't enjoy it. Even in the dark, barely touched by the timid moonlight, guilt haunted you like tradition. You shivered as if a ghost shot through you.

I've heard that if, after oral sex, your partner doesn't look like they've been exorcised, you're doing it wrong, but that's exactly how you looked and I *knew* I was doing it wrong.

Because everything we did was wrong—in your culture and mine, woman on woman, in darkness and in light.

"Let's get matching tattoos," I said when you rolled over and sunk into the hot pink and green serape on your bed. "Maybe ouroboros or something."

I said it slowly, drunkenly, stroking my rosy belly and then your coffee-colored one.

"You gringas could sell your parents into slavery and convince them it was a good idea."

Your voice was rough yet warbling, and I wondered how you could sound that way when you hadn't downed the beers or puffed the cigs I had. *Women who drink are putas. Women who smoke are putas.*

When I stared at your little mouth, you pushed away my circling pointer finger. Your short, bare nails brushed my lacquered black ones.

I shrugged my shoulders and said, "My mom has a tattoo. A butterfly on her ankle."

"My mom says tattoos are for putas," you said and then, after a pause, "Sometimes I think she wants to be a stereotype."

I chuckled. "Speaking for white people, I don't think there's a single one of us who wants to dance the way we dance." I bobbed my head and waved my arms as goofily as I could.

Instead of laughing, you sat up and locked eyes with me in your usual intense way. "But you want the good stereotypes. You want college and marriage and picket fences."

I nodded. "Sometimes."

"Mexicans want the good ones, too. The faith. The work ethic."

"No putas."

"No putas," you repeated. "But putas are like mermaids—they're still part human. Maybe more than that."

We sat on the serape, legs dangling over the bed like mermaids' fins dangle from seashore rocks. I thought about the mermaid found on a beach in Veracruz last summer, the one that, according to the Spanish-language media, turned out to be a creation of the "Pirates of the Caribbean" special effects team. I wondered if her sculptor had imagined her gay or straight, bisexual or asexual, puta or non-puta.

"My turn?" I asked, finally breaking the silence.

Your answer involved pushing me on my back and pressing your face to the wet warmth between my legs, in the dark, barely touched by the timid moonlight.

One Suitcase

You spend your spare moments in Virginia office parks
       perusing apartment galleries in New York City.
Your phone is a forest of bookmarks.
Your web history is one myopic dream of Bushwick or Harlem.
You pluck each listing—a forbidden fruit—while your boss
              masturbates in his corner office
       and drop it an ongoing email chain to yourself.

Someone will have to die before you get a theater job here.
Almost all of the theatre employees have technically retired.
They toiled away for the federal government for decades
       and found a second career on or behind stage,
       entertaining out-of-state tourists
              who've come to see Civil War battlefields.
These plays never have any black characters,
       except for the occasional Mammy or Uncle Tom.
These are not the plays you hope to make.

You keep an empty suitcase under your bed,
       so your mother won't stumble into your room and see it.
She would hate to know that you are unhappy,
       even though she already *knows*.
       Before the office parks, before theatre school,
              you were a biracial girl in the South.

The suitcase is vintage and leather,
a prop for a student film you designed.
A yellow-and-blue plaid silk lines the interior.
Its secret compartment makes you giddy.
You always loved secrets.
This suitcase is your secret.
New York City is your secret.
And one day you intend to fill this suitcase,
for the longer it remains empty,
the emptier your heart becomes.

The Mystery of My Height

I am as tall as a Colonialist
    but that's not my full story
If I fall in love with you
    I may invite you to
        read my genealogy
        in an unmade bed
        by a roaring fire
          the flames illuminating
          the pages of my shame
We can try to re-write our ancestors' biographies
    but they lived long before we breathed
        our cunts and cocks nowhere near creation
          let alone maturation
          our fucking only a dream
            they were too hungry to imagine
You say all you want to know is how tall our children will be
    and I say I do not know
        I can only guess
Genetics are always a wild guessing game
    among my people
    because we are all mixed up
    like the pebbles in riverbeds

The Chinatown Bus

The day your boss asked you to give him a foot massage
 is the day you bought a bus ticket to New York.
You quit simply by walking out, leaving no letter.
 Fuck him and his ilk.
 Fuck him and his bowtie.
 Fuck him and his Hampden-Sydney diploma.
 You don't care if he's a "Southern gentleman."
 You are not his Sally Hemings.

You whip out the suitcase from under your bed
 and fill it with the tattered sweaters of your theater school days.
 Fare thee well, Ann Taylor.
You are no office professional.
You are a street urchin ready to roam Manhattan for a few weeks
 until Broadway scoops you up
 and hires you to design costumes for all the stars.

The Chinatown bus pulls up in a Richmond alleyway at 1 a.m.
 The driver rips your ticket out of your hand
  and you stumble down the aisle in search of a seat.
   It stinks of stir-fry and mildew and weed.
After they board, everyone immediately pretends to fall asleep.
They cannot actually be asleep because the bus shakes
 like the last of the newborn calves in the field to walk.
 This is the most country you have felt in a long time.

You close your eyes and think about
    how your parents do not know you are on this bus.
You told them you were staying with a friend in Richmond.
    All they heard was you wanted to relive your college glory days.
They did not imagine you took an Uber from Fredericksburg
    to run away to a city they visited once 20 years ago.

It would've been easier if the bus left from your hometown
    because seeing Richmond makes your heart ache.
When you lived there, you spent every day dreaming of theatre.
    You knew nothing of the 9-to-5 grind and bad office coffee.
    You didn't have a boss, only professors who lived to inspire.

After the bus pulls to the side of the road in Baltimore
    And two men emerge from the woods
    to load on dozens of garbage bags
    you, too, pretend to fall asleep.
The Big Apple lights will wake you in three hours.

Un/whole

My clam ear does not exist in mirrors.
My clam ear does not exist in photographs.
I pull a curtain of hair over it
    to shade it,
    to protect it
because it is incomplete,
    unwhole,
    half-shelled,
    a delicacy for sharks
no one can devour me but me.

Couchsurfing in Bushwick

When you step off of the Chinatown bus, snow covers your curly head.

    It's winter in New York and so much colder than you expected.

You do not come from people who endure the winter chill well.

Your father emerged from his mother already a bayou man,

no time for boyhood when you're born black in the South.

    He could shrimp before he could talk.

And your mama was one of those Tennessee Williams damsels,

    white and forlorn and desperate under the red sun.

You were made for porches and wiping sweat from your yellow brow.

    New York knows nothing of temperate December days.

You text someone from theater school that you hooked up with once or twice.

    You're not sure exactly because

    there were always one too many Kentucky Mules.

hey u up? can i crash with u? in nyc now

    At 8 a.m. on Saturday, he could still be sleeping.

    If he's not, you don't mind if he confuses this for a booty call.

You just need shelter until Broadway notices your talent.

In a year, you'll have a Tony and a Chelsea penthouse.

Maybe you'll design J. Lo's costume in that *Bye Bye Birdie* remake.

    You just have to hustle.

    You just have to *not* go back to Virginia.

You glance at the skyscrapers engulfing 34ᵗʰ Street

and the naked trees—more naked than any tree in Fredericksburg.

Let the panic subside and you may have a chance at survival.

yeah i'm up. come over. 248 mckibbin st, bk.

bk?

brooklyn

Brooklyn?

      You thought only gangsters lived in Brooklyn.

         Was Theo a gangster?

         He looked like Jared Leto.

ok what's your subway stop?

morgan ave on the L

You fumbled with your phone as you determined your route.

It would be too many stops before you landed in Bushwick.

There would be too many men standing on the corner,

      asking to be your *papi, mamacita.*

      Wasn't it too early for that question?

When you tiptoe past a big drunk man to grab a bodega breakfast sandwich,

you sigh and think, *This is why my father can't wear a hoodie anywhere.*

The Worst Slumber Party

When you share your room with your sister, every night is a slumber party—at least when you edit out the spats. Nostalgia deletes the memory of her slashing your homecoming dress junior year and you cutting off a chunk of her hair in return. You have no recollection of her using your favorite lipstick to draw a line down the center of the room (allotting herself the bigger half.) You definitely don't remember her selling your underwear to middle school boys the minute she started high school.

Once Mami called lights out, all had been forgiven. "Never, ever go to bed angry," she used to say much like her mother before her, the same cock to her oblong head.

What you do remember are the nights you and your sister clutched each other close well past bedtime. You giggled about cartoons, crushes, and all the worst teachers. Your sister's hair smelled like cinnamon and her eyes were really gray, even if most everyone called them blue. She always pulled your curls, watching them spring back into place and laughing every time. In return, you called her Mud Pie because her skin was so much darker than yours— but only ever in the cocoon of your room. At school, she was Mariela, just as Mami had named her. Never Mari and *definitely* never Mud Pie.

Back then, you shared a bed because Mami said they didn't come free. Really, it wasn't a bed. It was a mattress, threadbare and off-color, the same indescribable shade of bubblegum that's been living on the sidewalk too long but not quite long enough to be black. The mattress was so warped and worn that you woke up every morning with backaches and the two of you constantly stole the blanket from each other. One sister wrapped herself up while the other curled up and shivered, not wanting to wake the burrito. She looked so peaceful.

But Mud Pie promised the bed famine was a temporary challenge for the Gomez sisters. All great heroines must suffer sometimes.

"Because I'm going to college," said Mariela. "After I graduate, I'm going to make so much money that all of us will have our own beds. Huge ones with headboards and even throw pillows. Gotta have throw pillows when you're rich."

A beat later, she added, "You're going to college, too."

You nod because you are three years younger than her. Then you close your eyes and dream like any other night.

Soon after that, Mariela is talking about college instead of cartoons and crushes. She lights up when she shows you the admissions brochures. She even brings them to your sorry mattress so you can pour over them together.

"They all kind of look the same," you say more than once as you peruse page after page of manicured lawns and large, imposing buildings. You toss aside the brochures from less picturesque schools.

"No, *mira*, this one is all stone. This one is all brick," she replied one night as she piled more brochures on your lap. "Besides, that's not even what matters."

"But don't you want to go to a pretty one or, like, one by the beach?"

"I'm not going to college to *party*."

You shrug and tug for a bigger share of the blanket. "Your loss."

Night after night, you fall asleep among piles of brochures. More than once you wonder if they'd be a more effective cover than your threadbare blanket.

Mari wrote essays, ran to the copy shop, printed this and that, and cursed too loudly when she messed something up because she knew Mami worked hard for the money.

"These applications are so expensive," she muttered as you waited in line with her at the bank. Everyone there had clothes that look catalog-fresh, not like they fished them out of a donation box at the church down the block.

A year later, Mari is at a college among cornfields. You weren't home the afternoon her acceptance letter arrived. She sobbed by herself at the kitchen counter when she read the part about her full-ride. You were making out behind the dilapidated tennis courts at school, learning how someone else's teeth are supposed to feel.

Once Mari shipped off to school, you had the bedroom to yourself. You wiped off the lipstick divider between your side and her side, and spread out your meager belongings. Dust bunnies grew because Mari was not there to clean them. And sometimes, at night, instead of texting your friends, you cried hot tears because you missed Mud Pie. You knew Mami heard you as she did her crossword puzzles in the next room over, but she never came to console you. The next morning, you would eat frozen waffles together in silence—that is if you caught sight of your maternal ghost at all.

It wasn't until winter howled through Phoenix that you and Mari were reunited, but her eyes are stormy and her head hangs low, as if permanently bowed due to some monastic vow. When you slid into bed that first night together, she nuzzled your shoulder like an infant.

"What's the matter?" you asked, wanting to wiggle away but knowing to stay still, stiller than she was in that moment of absolute quiet.

"I'm not going back," she finally uttered. You go cold.

"You have to go back. You're the smart one. You have a full scholarship."

She whispered darkly, "I'm going to tell you a secret." Then she turned away from you. "I was raped at a party."

And all the sounds of Phoenix that you always hated—the screechy birdsongs, the intrusive insects, the insufferable desert wind, even the gunshots and the car horns—seemed to collide into a cacophony amplified by Mud Pie's wailing.

When the prickly pear cacti bloomed that spring, Mari was still home. She relinquished her scholarship, took up waitressing, and bought two beds by the end of the year.

A Baby Girl

The nurses shrouded the infant in pink
    because by the nurture of her sex
        {not its nature}
    her freedom had already shriveled
        up inside of her mother's warm womb
          {the last true refuge}.

The moment she breathed her first earthly breath
    the stench of sexism stung her hummingbird nostrils
          {male doctors belittling female nurses}
          {slap / pinch / mansplain}.
What life was left for this tiny girl to live
    when the world conspired to make her feel tinier & tinier
    as soon as she reached the hospital room?

You, girl child, are biggest now as a newborn, still fluttering in naivety
    before they pluck off your wings & throw you in the dirt.
          {*Stay down*, they hiss, *stay down*.}
      You'll want to laugh at the irony
        from the tangles of mud & slime
        where you'll forever be imprisoned—
      but you can't
        when you're choking on tears & wondering why
        they hate you for what God made you.

My Mother's Pantsuit

My mother did not abandon her whole world as she knew it
    and furrow her brow into the telltale wrinkles of a fretting immigrant
    and agonize over take-home practice tests printed on cheap newsprint
    and hole herself up in the public library to suffer in profound silence
    and pour over every scrap and tome of English text within her reach
    and question if there would be room left for any Spanish in her brain
    and read dictionaries and encyclopedias forward and backward
    and sharpen her No. 2 pencils to crisp points like tiny knives
    and don her best silk blouse and pantsuit à la Hillary
    and sit for an exam she was terrified of failing
    and recite an oath that made her knees shake
just for a racist xenophobe to occupy la Casa Blanca.

Apartment Hunting

Theo lived with six roommates.
Half of them thought you were black;
half of them thought you were white.
In the month you found refuge on his sofa,
not one of them ever asked, but you could
read their interpretation based on
how they discussed the pricklier points of race.
None of them had been to Virginia, save for one.
He once shot past Washington, D.C. and
spent a couple of hours in Arlington
before he realized his mistake.
He said the Potomac looked ferocious,
but you were a Rappahannock River girl.
You still didn't know the bodies of water
that threatened to swallow New York.
In Bushwick, the only drops you saw
lined the gutter and pooled on the sidewalk.
Sometimes the cry of seagulls pricked your ears.
A little lost, the birds had not steered too far off course.
But you never mentioned nature to your unwilling neighbors.
"Lavinia," said Theo one morning, while lighting a joint,
"It's been nice, but you have to find an apartment.
Craigslist that shit, girl. It's not *that* sketch."
You stopped chewing your grits (a remnant of home)

and nodded slower than a late-night G train.

"It's all run together," you say. "I forgot how long I was here."

"This city sweeps you up, but you learn to fight it."

He exhales and you both appreciate the clouds he fashions.

"Where do you want to live?" he finally asks.

"Somewhere where I can see the sky," you say, surprising yourself.

"Welcome to Brooklyn. No tunnels of building shadows here."

"As long as it's cheap," you say, thinking of closets and slums.

You don't add that you have nearly run out of savings

because Theo will try to convince you to work at his office,

the call center that lets him reschedule his shifts for auditions.

You didn't flee to New York to ooze in and out of a 9-to-5.

You didn't move here to dread every day of your existence.

You came here to revel in textiles, to dress Broadway's stars,

to tell stories through costumes like you dreamt in school.

"We'll look at listings and book appointments for tomorrow,"

says Theo in a daze now that the pot has hit him.

"Sure, load me up," you mutter and grab his joint.

It's your moment to escape, to surrender

as a speckled seagull shrieks outside.

Defining a Slut

But the boys—
    {you're a girl}
But the boys
    {you're *not* a boy}
But the boys—
    {you're a whore}
Because I—?
    {yes}
Because I—?
    {indeed}
Because I—?
    {without a doubt}
All I ever did was exist as a woman
    {slut, slut, slut}

The Sea of Social Media

There is no body positivity movement for clam ears.
There is no hashtag,

    no secret Facebook group,

    no scrolling Tumblr page.

I have navigated the entire sea of social media

    and I remain the lone mermaid

    tangled in the seaweed,

    ashamed of my half-shell.

Am I wicked for my deformity?
Will I ever have a chance to battle

    the sea witch who cursed me?

Is there no vengeance for those born like me?

Signing the Lease

Your parents still quiver with fear and rage
when they imagine you in New York City.
"Bedwick?" your father shouts on the phone.
"How come a neighborhood sounds like 'bed wet'?
Is that a *black* neighborhood?"
He sneers the second question
much harder than the first.
This coming from a man with green veins.
Your blue blood mother just doesn't understand
why you would want to live so far from
George Washington's boyhood home.
"There's a lovely dinner theater in Fredericksburg,"
says your mother on the other line
and you know she's staring at the creek
just beyond your old bedroom.
"You could work there, get an apartment downtown."
You imagine sewing petticoats and hoopskirts
for Southern belles over and over and over again.
Every play will retell the story of the Lost Cause
and you, the mulatto, will clench your teeth behind stage.
Slowly, your gums will start bleeding until one day
they are nothing but pulp jiggling on your jaw.
That is why you cannot return to Fredericksburg:
You will ruin your body, not to mention your soul.

After a few heated conversations with Mom and Dad,
they agree to co-sign your lease for a studio apartment
off of the Gates stop on the J Train, on Bushwick Avenue.
You can't pretend your address possesses much style,
but at least you can hoof it to the cool kids in 15 minutes.
Where you grew up in Virginia, you cannot walk anywhere,
except the meadow or the mill or the end of a long, long road.
Your father simply writes, "You'll come back" in the email
containing a signed PDF of the lease and you squirm.
A wisp of you yearns to smell a magnolia leaf
and listen to your backyard cardinals sing
because this place freezes in winter
and nobody sprinkles Old Bay
and you wonder if you are
as strong as you hoped.
But maybe you are
more cartilage
than bone.
You
still
sign.

Artist Statement

I pluck my hair from the root because my scalp can make the sacrifice. Because I want to create from my own body. Because my children are hungry.

Open the studio. There is no paint in the house. Open the fridge. There is no milk in the house. Open the cupboards. There is no bread in the house. We don't have eggs or peanut butter or carrots or canned beans or anything edible at all. We finished the last bag of corn chips before the weekend crept up and shook our shoulders in another one of its cruel tricks.

"I'm here," the weekend slithered. "Here to haunt you. Kill you."

At school, the children eat because there is some fairness in this world, or at least pity. My daughters line up in the cafeteria, fill their trays with permitted items, and punch in a special code when they step up to the register. Then they sit down and fill their stomachs. But at home, we have no special code.

There is no acrylic in the house and my children are hungry. There is no charcoal in the house and my children are hungry. There is no pastel in the house and my children are hungry.

But there is a bottle of glue at the back of my desk. Holy, holy, holy.

For canvas, I cut out a panel from a cereal box from the days when we had food. Then I stumble to the porch, the only place with ample light since I can't afford to replace half of the bulbs, and I begin pulling out my hair, strand by strand.

I crouch over the rail and yank until I have a handful of Titian strands. My hair is my paint.

From this hair I will craft a woman in my own image. She will possess the large, sore breasts of a woman still nursing. She will try to conceal the scarred vulva of a woman who has given a painful birth by arranging her black curls just so. Perhaps then a man will love her and stay. Perhaps then she will no longer carry the burden of feeding her children alone.

I tell myself all of this as I arrange and paste until I run out of strands. Then I twist, twirl, and tug yet again with the repetition of wiping a soiled child clean. I patch and paste over and over as my woman takes shape. My woman needs no other subject, no accessories, no objects in the foreground. My woman will hang in a gallery. May the whole city see the desperation in her red eyes. May the whole city feel the rumble of her stomach.

"What are you doing, Mommy?" comes a faint little voice. But I do not answer by opening my mouth. I answer inside my head:

I remember when you were born, Sarah. Your father and I had already split. I had nothing to eat. They gave me nothing at the hospital and there was nothing in the house. So I huddled on the crumbling porch and stared at the moon, thinking I could eat it if I stared long enough. The next day there was no food, either.

Finally, on your third day since leaving my womb, Grandma stopped by with two brown paper bags stuffed with groceries. It was pay day and she wanted to celebrate your life even if she hated your daddy almost as much as I did. I was huddled on the porch again, this time watching the neighborhood children play in the streets, wondering how many of them were hungry, too. I was sucking and pulling my hair because, even then, it was my bad habit. If I pulled out enough hair, maybe I would stop being hungry. Maybe all I would think of then would be my scalp stinging from the hurricane of my hand uprooting so many strands. Grandma almost toppled over when I charged her and seized the bags. I ate right there on the lawn: a green apple and chocolate pudding without a spoon.

Let's wait for this to dry. Then we'll catch the bus to the art gallery and hand in my lady of hair. Maybe someone will notice her and buy her. Maybe there will be food at the opening reception. Maybe then we will eat.

The Almost-Rape

my uncle got whatever he wanted

    so when he wanted me

        he assumed he'd get me

but there were thorns on this rosebud

    and when he touched me

        in the dampness of his basement

            with the mold as our only witness

    i didn't just scrape him

        i cut him deep

he told my mother that he fell down the stairs

    carrying too many odds & ends to donate to his parish

    his heart so heavy with charity that he stumbled

i didn't correct him during his telling of the flimsy tale

    because my mother would never trust my story

        and even if she did

            what of my virtue?

Daddy's Dollars

New York rent sucked the savings from your bank account
and poured them into the murky sea where all such money goes.
You just watched as your bills swirled and swum away.
Now you stand in your drained pool—desperate, forlorn.
How can it already be time to beg your parents for something?
You have no doubt that they can pay your Bushwick rent for a year.
Daddy remains one of the highest-ranked black men in the Army
and Mother sits on a grand tobacco and Christmas tree fortune.
The questions that feed the shame growing in your heart are:
Will they rescue you out of kindness? Or will they say being
a biracial girl is no plight in Brooklyn? Why haven't you
abandoned your tragic mulatto narrative and learned
discipline? Why are you as stuck here as you were in
Virginia? Why can't you take care of yourself for
once? But you squelch the shame and make
the call you hope will not ruin you.
You have been cursed with a
weak cell connection in
your stinky studio,
so you dodge
from spot
to spot.
"Dad?"

You finally hear him pick up and now you wonder if you made
a mistake, thinking you could trust him with your fragility,
your desperation, your confession that you cannot buy
dinner, let alone breakfast tomorrow or the day after.
Then you launch into you plea because you have no
time for pleasantries, since you must know how
you will eat, how you will afford a warmer coat,
how you will pay the rent due in ten days.
Daddy is surprisingly docile and agrees
to zap you a couple thousand dollars
over the Internet, on the condition
that you email him your resume
and a sample cover letter
that very same night.
He says he needs
proof that you
are trying
and hangs
up.

A Purity Ball Fashion Statement

She always hated white dresses
    but nobody asked her opinion
    and you can't wear red
    to a purity ball
So, she wore pink
    because she saw no shame
    in having nearly tainted waters
Besides, it reminded her of a blush
    And blushing at least was something
      she was allowed to do
        even in the light of day
          when the sun seemed to reveal all
          and the only secrets were the ones
          we chose not to see

Comfort in Swimming

I am alive by the sea,
    in the sea,
        a recluse in the waves,
        but a vibrant recluse.
I express myself in laps,
    inhabiting bubbles and breaths.
You cannot catch me because
    I do not wish to be caught.
There is no net wide enough,
        deep enough,
        hungry enough.
There is no net with jaws.
I am the one with jaws.
I am the one wide enough,
        deep enough,
        hungry enough.
Water has transformed my body.
Water has washed over me,
    washed over my worries,
    washed over my deformities,
        mental deformities,
        physical deformities,
        spiritual deformities.
I am not the woman with the crushed ear.
I am the woman with a soul like the ocean.

Courtship As a Virgin c. 2016

"You have to put that you're waiting for marriage on your Tinder."

"Why?"

"To weed out anyone who considers that a deal-breaker."

"What if a guy changes his mind once he meets me?"

"If it's really a deal-breaker, he won't change his mind."

"Even if he falls in love with me?"

"He might fall in love with you, but you'll have no future."

"You can't be sure of that."

"Don't you think it's more likely I'm right than not?"

Costume Warehouse Dreams

Somehow you tricked someone into employing you.

On your first day, you show up at the costume warehouse
in a black leather jacket with pants to match because this is New York.
Never mind that you will be populating spreadsheets
and handling paperwork day in and day out.
You will look glamorous doing it, dammit.

You could never be the fresh-eyed blonde
they find so pretty in Virginia, but here
in the Big Apple, you can be edgy and edgy surpasses pretty.

You refuse to cover your high-yellow complexion
with too-light foundation and powder.
You line your eyes in kohl to make them appear even blacker.
Then you apply (and re-apply) lip gloss so your lips appear even fuller.
To hell with anyone who thinks them too full.
You are biracial and you will not soften your blackness.
You are biracial and you will not privilege your whiteness.

After you've put on your armor, you're ready for the battle
of production assistants who will swamp you for everything
on the checklists their bosses handwrote on scrap paper at midnight,
at their kitchen table, while they clutched their third glass of wine.

You know this because of the burgundy spots and smeared ink.

You feel powerful as you glance at the P.A.s' pleading faces,
knowing you could get them fired or help them secure that promotion.
And that is the most powerful you have felt in a very long time.
You use that power for good because benevolence has bitten you.

You have a job in your industry in New York City, among bright lights.
You are contributing to theater, to film, to television watched everywhere.
This isn't the dream, but you can feel the steppingstone firmly under your feet.

Now staple Form A to Form B, stamp them both, and file them away.

Costume Warehouse Nightmares

You have stapled many Form A's to many Form B's
and you want to consume every production assistant's hope
in a single, furious gulp with your big, tired mouth.

You didn't haul ass to New York City to hole yourself up in an LIC cave,
working as a glorified secretary, doing more paper-clipping than sewing.

Your fingers are stale. Your mind is stale. Your heart is stale.
Weren't you put on this earth to design for Broadway's stars?
Weren't you meant to be a costume whisperer? A textile queen?

Once you were a biracial girl rotting in a Virginia office park.
Now you are a biracial girl rotting in a Queens warehouse.
These are two different forms of torture, two different ways
to fade, to disappear, to vanish into the Invisible Woman.

In theatre school, you never hear about these dingy corners.
You never hear about all of the clipboards you will clutch.
You never hear about all of the snobs and sloths whose murder
you will plot in quieter moments because your professors
are too busy feeding on their own nostalgia, resenting
their own failures, planning their next show,
fantasizing about the glory that is retirement.

There is no glamor in retirement, but there is a pension.

You have no benefits at the warehouse job.
The benefit is that you're employed,
that your parents will let you stay
in the Big Apple as long as you
have a source of income.

That's how low the bar has been set.
You can afford Lean Cuisines.

Never mind your desire to tell
the kinds of stories
they would never
allow back home.

Street Corner Mangos

The lady who sells mangos on the street
    reminds me of my mother and her kitchen,
        where a pot of beans always boils on the stove
        y el queso fresco siempreestámuy fresco.

My mother holes herself up *en sucocina* 226 miles south of here,
    where federal government employees pound the sidewalks.
And I am the little beggar artist, thieving in the night.
    Hear me recite a poem. Mind the hat on the sidewalk.
        Buy a painting, any painting. I have many more
            if you want to see them.
    I wish I could buy all of the mangos,
    but I have to hustle like the mango lady, too.

The Red Sea

Daddy stood at the yellowed porcelain sink, staring at my stained Hello Kitty panties. I had never seen this man—the direct descendant of the first Scotch-Irish settler to take down an elk in the Shenandoah Valley in 1715—so small and wilted. He hunched over the basin and rubbed his face with his sunburned hands.

Meanwhile, I stood in the bathroom doorway of our illegally converted carriage house, looking at him looking at my soiled, soggy panties. I was thirteen and, twenty years later, can still feel my mortification in that moment.

"Look, Katie," he finally said, "if I can clean out the coffee stains from my work shirts, I can clean this."

I slowly nodded, taking a moment to study his mottled face ten shades lighter than mine as I began chipping the paint on the doorframe.

"But blood and coffee aren't the same, Daddy," I said.

He closed his eyes and sighed. "What time does the library close?"

"It's Sunday."

"Dammit. Well, I'll go to the one in Carytown tomorrow and search for, I don't know, *tips* on the Internet. There's gotta be other dads who—"

"Dad, it's OK. We'll just let the soap sit." I accidentally tore off too big a chip of paint, making a surprisingly loud *craaack*. "But, um, what about the...?"

We locked eyes and I could see him thinking, *Don't say tampon.*

"You know." I uttered at long last. All of Richmond must've shaken from the momentous rumble of my words.

"Uh, well, I'm sure Mrs. Collins is home. We could knock on her door."

Mrs. Collins was our widowed 89-year-old neighbor. She and her husband had moved here back when the neighborhood was still considered a "good" one by uptight white suburbanites. I liked her because she never made me feel strange for having a white dad. But even as a seventh-grader, I knew Mrs. Collins had been menopausal for longer than I'd been alive.

"You sure she remembers how to use a you-know-what?"

Dad's face broke into a smile. "I bet it's like riding a bicycle," he said. "You never forget how to do it."

A couple minutes later, we waited on Mrs. Collins' porch as she made her way to the door with glacial pace. While I blocked the rest of the memory, I do know Mrs. Collins told me to try sanitary napkins first and she just so happened to have a diaper-size pad.

The following afternoon, Dad put a print-out with tips for menstrual blood removal on the 'fridge, but I didn't see it until later because I was trawling the streets with Marty Monogue, a white boy who also went to Binford Middle but lived in a different neighborhood.

When we had enough of chasing stray cats and peering through people's windows, he turned to me and asked, "Wanna go to Texas Beach?"

I shrugged. "I guess. The frogs should still be out."

"Yeah, we should put some in my mom's dresser before dinner."

Twenty minutes later, after hiking down a steep hill and crossing the train tracks, we were on the silty shore of the James River and I immediately spotted my first frog jumping in the reeds. In a single lunge, I caught it. The frog was small and brown and scared as I cupped it.

"Way to go, Katie!" Marty said and slapped me so hard on the back that I stumbled forward, scattering pebbles into the water. The frog instantly peed and warmed up my hands.

"Hey, watch it," I muttered.

"Sorry. Wanna go swimming?" he said all in one breath.

"We don't have bathing suits."

"So? You have underwear, right?"

I blushed in response. Then I noticed Marty's elfin eyes glued to my left thigh.

"Katie..."

I glanced down to find a large drop of blood determined to reach my ankle.

"You're bleeding!"

"No, I'm not," I shouted and pushed him, still clutching the frog in one hand.

He pushed me back and yelled, "You're disgusting!"

"Shut up!" Another push.

"No, you're gross!" Yet another push.

"No, I'm not. This happens to all girls, stupid!" Fighting tears, I backed up, threw the frog at him, and raced back up the hill before I could even tell if I had hit him.

When I fell, I tore at rocks and roots to get back up. Marty didn't follow me.

I ran all the way to my bathroom to shower and change my pad. Then I planted myself on the sagging sofa and starved until Dad swung by with McD's before he went back to work.

"Your mom always wanted McDonald's when it was her time of month," he said.

As I tore through my McDouble and small fries, I vowed that Marty and I would never talk again. I briefly wondered if the frog I threw at him had died and if Mom would've thrown the frog, too.

"Probably not," I said to myself, sitting in the dark now that the sun had set. Dad still hadn't changed the lightbulb in the living room. So, as the crickets' song descended upon Rosewood Avenue, my mind wandered to Randolph Pool around the block.

I pictured myself hitting the pavement barefoot, darting out from the streetlights to return to the shadows until I turned right to cut through an alley. When I reached the fence circling the pool, I surveyed my surroundings before starting my ascent. Even when my knee snagged a loose wire, I kept going. When I got inside, I immediately began stripping. I balled up my sanitary napkin, tossed it to the ground, and sprung into a cannonball. My splash created a tsunami. I came up for a deep breath of air, exhaled, and floated on my back as my menses gradually snaked its way out of me and danced with the cyan waves. I didn't leave until the chlorine burned my nostrils, my fingertips were raisins, and the pool was crimson.

Sleeping like a Flounder

I slept on my beautiful side.

I never slept on my clam ear.

I left it open to the sea.

I did not want the weight of my skull to crush it further.

I could only tolerate a deformity so deformed.

Let the bubbles and waves serenade it, I thought.

May the seaweed dance for you, I crooned.

The fish will swish in tune for you

and the coral will handle the harmony.

Even the anemones add to the lullaby.

This is the song of the ocean, clam ear.

This Is Why

I crumple on the exam table, feeling small and dusty like a battered moth. Eventually the grease on my body began to congeal after days of not showering. Now I am coated. When the doctor re-enters the room, I will myself to perk up, to appear less wilted. I may be here because I'm unwell, but I don't have to look unwell, I tell myself. I have my pride. Perhaps not full-fledged confidence, but pride, a pride that is as stubborn as I am.

"So," the doctor says, as she looks me up and down. "Menstrual problems?"

She is a small, plump Salvadoran woman with freckles. So is my mother. They both have the same liquid brown eyes and thick, dark hair. My gaze rests on the doctor's full lips as my hands fall to my stomach.

"Yeah," I say. "My cramps are really bad."

The doctor raises an eyebrow. "How bad?"

I shrug and stutter, "I-I d-don't know. Bad?" My voice rises when I wish it wouldn't. Now my intonation has ruined everything. I am the moth pinned to the board. Stuck. Am I not already helpless enough, being a 19-year-old woman, an immigrant's daughter in a land of Confederate generals' descendants?

Then she asks the question I knew she would ask, the question she was responsible for asking, the question I dreaded.

"Well, what are you taking?"

My head is swirling, my stomach is swirling, my whole

body is swirling, except for my abdomen, which is burning, and I just want to scream, but I am a moth and moths do not scream.

"Nothing."

"Nothing?"

"Nothing."

"No painkillers? Motrin? Midol? Aleve? A generic ibuprofen?"

I shake my head. My mind skips to the agonizing girl curled up in bed yesterday. Then it flashes to my grandmother clinging to the sofa in San Salvador, taking another swig of Tíck Táck and popping another pill. She is as grubby as I am, but older, drunker, sadder. It has been almost a week since she left that sofa, almost a week since she was raped again. She took an icy shower to wash away the blood after the attack and has not showered since then. When she finally pulls herself off the sofa, my grandmother walks to the kitchen, downs 60 tablets of ibuprofen, drenches herself in kerosene, and lights herself on fire. My mother is the age I am now, and at work when it happens. She is always working, except for those five days she takes off to sit at my grandmother's side in the hospital. On the fifth day, the abuela I never had dies.

"No," I mutter as I stare at the doctor's right shoulder, afraid that if I meet her eyes, I will cry. "I do not take painkillers." I do not tell her that my mother kept the ibuprofen locked up in our house. It was simpler not to take painkillers at all than to have to ask my mother permission. Even at college, my mother's stern expression and questioning.

"You must take Motrin," she says firmly. "It will make the suffering much easier."

She is referring to a different kind of suffering than I feel in that moment, the physical manifestation of my womanhood, not the burden of my family history. Suddenly I tense up the way I do when classmates offer me alcohol at parties. My muscles get so tight that it hurts, and I'm the moth willing itself to camouflage with the bark on the tree beneath its spindly legs. Yet I am not hiding. I am in plain sight of my doctor. I exhale and my muscles relax. I meet her eyes and say much more calmly than I thought possible, "Addiction runs in my family."

The doctor's face softens. "I understand, but if you take the painkillers exactly as directed, you should be fine. You will not get addicted. Just follow the directions on the bottle."

"What if I take more?"

"Don't take more."

"But what if I do?"

"You won't," she says. "It's a huge help that you know your family history. You're aware and you'll be cautious. Take painkillers only as prescribed and it will be all fine."

Fine. All fine. The words ring and the scene of my grandmother on the sofa goes black.

The doctor pats my hand when I don't respond.

"Right after this, I want you to go to the drugstore and buy a bottle of ibuprofen," she says. "Come back next month if you still can't manage the pain, but you must do this first."

I nod.

"Promise?"

"Yes."

"You'll go the store and you'll take the pills and you'll be fine." The doctor's voice is faint and echoing at this point.

"Fine."

"Good. Now off you go."

"Thank you."

"Of course. Bye now."

When I walk out of the exam room, I have the wings not of a moth but a butterfly. And a couple of hours later, as I stand in the shower, I notice that the cramps have lessened. At least one kind of suffering has ended.

One Year in New York

The past ten months have been the same,
save for the weather, your outfits, and the Tinder men.
The seasons here are harsher than in Virginia.
Your outfits, while always black, change in length and fabric.
Since you buy your lipgloss on clearance, the color never
remains the same from month to month.
Sometimes, your Tinder dates are blonde.
Sometimes, your Tinder dates are brunette.
Once, your Tinder date was bald—very bald.
Otherwise, the past ten months truly have been the same.

You tear yourself out of bed early and shower early
and dress early and eat early and catch the train early.
When you get to the costume warehouse, you clock in
and swiftly sneak over to the bodega for Cuban coffee.
Then you return and the production assistants descend
upon you with their wardrobe requests for this Broadway
show and that slick commercial and that movie slated for
next Christmas *so make sure you have enough jingle bells.*
Fill out Form A and now Form B. Stamp. Stamp. And staple.
For lunch, you grab pepperoni pizza, a green apple, and Sprite.
You scroll through Tinder, maybe send a message here and there.
More clamoring production assistants mean more orders to fill,
so you fill them and sweep up stray sequins at the end of the day.

Repeat that schedule, Monday through Friday, with weekend dates.
One year. A year. One whole year. Twelve months total.
One month of couch-surfing. One month of job-hunting.
Whether you will see rats copulating on the subway that day
is the only unpredictable factor anymore, but even that's 50-50.
Either way, you are not designing costumes for the stars.

La frontera entre El Salvador y Virginia

from coffee plantation to tobacco plantation
a visa & a plane ticket
    to escape the slaughter
    for the silence of suburbia
    where all the houses have the same bones

there is no cure-all for the immigrant's broken heart

the flavors of a new country will taste foreign
    for as long as you let them linger on your tongue
    & dwell upon the tastes of your long-ago homeland

you filled out thickets of papers to be reunited with your husband
    who left a nation pockmarked by war
    to wash dishes in a restaurant he couldn't afford

this november, you will not let *him* spit on your struggle
    that is why you're with *her*
        voting with blood

Sea Cave

Sometimes, I hide in the dark

because the other mermaids shine too bright

like coins dropped in the sea, reflecting a cruel sun.

I cower in the light, the heat,

the pressure to be beautiful, perfect.

In my cave, there is no light, no heat,

only blackness, iciness.

I shiver alone,

shrouded from scrutiny.

I could only be more hidden if

a squid enveloped me in a cloud of ink

and sometimes, I wish that would happen

to cloud my clam ear,

to render it invisible,

even if I could still see it in my mind's eye.

Mouse House

You carefully arranged each piece of straw, each stolen shoelace, each scrap of newspaper. Mama Mouse wanted her nest. She wanted to burrow deep into that hovel on Clay Street and cozy up to her mate. The love will come, she said, The babies will come. All my dreams will flourish.

But the love never came and the babies never came and there was no flourishing of dreams. They festered instead. When you scurried away to build your nest elsewhere, I cried because you were alone. Mice are not meant to live alone. But sometimes sister mice must live apart.

I remember the headline from *Medscape Medical News*: "Mice Can Avoid Menopause, But Can Women?" Back when I edited copy for the hospital, I ran into more pregnant women on a daily basis than there were people in my high school graduating class. That's what I get for growing up in Appalachia but living and working in Norfolk. Too far from Richmond to snuggle with you and gnaw on wood.

I had my own nest in Ghent, a warm one not built *for* love but *by* love. Papa Mouse loved me and I loved Papa Mouse. We were getting on like mice in love do, so we knew we'd be not two but three soon.

There's a Yahoo! Answers thread called "Our mice buried their dead cagemate ...?" It reminds me of how I had to bury my happiness under the cage litter, that way you wouldn't see it. That way you wouldn't think of how your buck mouse had found another doe.

"I still have stuff at our house," you said one night while we sat on the porch, making fun of the passing marathon runners. Purple and gray tinted the shadows beneath your eyes. You wore no makeup and your hair jumped out like Einstein's. You hadn't showered in days.

"*His* house. This is your house now," I said.

"You know what I mean."

"Use the right words: 'me,' 'my,' 'I.' No more 'we' and 'our'."

"Can you stop being a big sister for five seconds?"

I chugged my root beer and threw the bottle in the recycling bin by your swing.

"Give me the key," I said.

"What?"

"The key to his place."

"Why?"

"I'm going to get the rest of your stuff. That way you never have to go into that damn apartment again."

"I can take care of it myself."

"I don't care if you can. I care that you don't." I kicked the recycling bin. Bottles crashing against one another filled the silence between us.

"It's like all the other breakups before," I said, much lower than before. "You'll get through it."

"I'm getting old." Fear flashed in your eyes.

I kneeled down and patted your hand. "All of us are. But you will love again. You are strong and you are beautiful."

You looked down at your lap and whispered, "Thank you." Then you stood up and fetched the key from your purse. You placed it in the palm of my hand and hugged me long enough for a few runners to stumble by.

"You know," you started as you pulled away and collapsed on the porch swing. "You'll never be able to carry all that stuff by yourself. I mean, there's not too much left, but it's heavy."

I shrugged. "I'm going to call Judy to help me. She's not doing anything today."

So I did. Judy agreed. All it took was the promise of food.

Judy and I nearly kicked his door down since the lock was ancient and rusty. When nobody answered, I forced the key one more time. The lock clicked. He wasn't home.

We scampered up the stairs, nearly tripping over a stack of pizza boxes and PBR cans. Your former bedroom looked like a crime scene. Drawing supplies, condoms, stuffed animals, and dirty clothes made up one foul-smelling potpourri.

Judy glanced at me.

"Let's put shit in garbage bags and come back for the chairs," I muttered.

Later that afternoon, we piled your living room high with our finds while you hung out with friends on the other side of town. Judy and I split a rotisserie chicken from the corner store before she split. I scrawled you a note and tucked it under your pillow. New nest, new dreams.

After tossing his key in the James River, I hit 64. I missed Papa Mouse and Papa Mouse missed me.

The next morning, I rolled over to quit my phone alarm and scroll through the web news. Apple and Facebook were encouraging their female employees to freeze their eggs, and all the bloggers were wondering which companies would follow. We never talked about it. For now, we will remove "freeze" from your vocabulary. Your nest can't stand to get any colder.

Praise for Mermen

Mermaids should fixate on the sea,
    embrace their power,
    sing to the anemone,
    wander through reefs,
    discover all the gems.
Not sit in anguish before the mirror.

The encouragement,
    while generous,
fails to recognize that mermen
    are praised for adventure
and mermaids
    are praised for their reflection.

Hugging Coral

Sometimes, my perception
of myself,
of my imperfection,
of my deformity,
incapacitates me.

My ugliness has frozen me in the sea.
I am trapped in a block of ice,
but I can see all of the fish swim by.
I have no companions in this block of ice.

I get so lonely, I wish I could hug coral.
Even a rock or a barnacle could sustain me.

Tell me I am beautiful.
Tell me I am worthy.
Tell me I am loved.

The Resignation

Here your New York City adventure comes to an end.

You have begged your Bushwick slumlord to fix the boiler one too many times.
You can no longer distinguish one Tinder match from another.
You don't have the strength to feign interest in any more Williamsburg brunches.
You find zero novelty in the sight of rats fucking on the subway tracks.
You have come to realize that one bodega is essentially the same as the next.
You are tired of explaining to distant relatives that Long Island City is Queens.
You are tired of hearing distant relatives say Archie Bunker was from Queens.
You hate how many tourists trample through Central Park.
You resent how little time you spend in Central Park.

Sometimes you look out onto Bushwick Avenue and stifle a scream.
Sometimes you bite your inner cheek while waiting for the G train.
Sometimes your inner cheek bleeds and you swallow the blood to feel alive.

You're not sure why New York is the setting for so many love stories.
You're not sure why you ever thought this was a place you could fall in love.
You're not sure why you ever thought this was a place you could tell stories.

When the costume warehouse is not busy, you could hear a ghost pass through.
Since your boss never drops by, you sometimes imagine you work for a ghost.
On the morning you resign, you imagine yourself writing a letter to a ghost.
There are no production assistants, only your dark, pickling thoughts.

But you cannot leave those, so you say you are resigning for personal reasons. You place the note behind the front desk and search for bus rides to Virginia. Maybe an office in Fredericksburg will hire a failed costume designer.

When You Loved Me in the Cornfield

I

You told me that I was sweet corn
and you were chaff
because my skin was lighter,
because my hair was straighter,
because your daddy chose a white wife.

II

I never dreamt of becoming a scarecrow
when I grew up—
whiling away the hours in the fields,
shaking the stalks
as we shook each other's bodies.

III

I met your mother exactly once
and wondered how
she didn't get lost
in the snow.

IV

When you asked me if
I would ever grow anything,
I thought you meant crops.
You meant wings.

V

Your father said it was a miracle
that he was raising a mulatto daughter
in the state that brought Loving
to the Supreme Court.

VI

That summer, we only
ate oysters—
yours,
mine,
and the Chesapeake's.

VII

Half a century ago,
we could have married
based on race,
but less than two years ago
based on sex.

VIII

Virginia's indigenous people
once ground oyster shells
for fertilizer.

IX

When you asked me if
I thought you looked
more black or white,
I said, "Both."

X

I never asked you if
you would wear
a white dress
or a tux.

XI

You told me that the
perfect sandy loam
is hard to find,
much like the
perfect woman.

XII

"I don't want to be a farmer"
was my repeated refrain.
"I don't want to be a half-breed"
was yours.

XIII

Was my skin too light?
Was my hair too straight?
Did I remind you of what
you didn't have?

XIV

Now the field is silent,
no longer heaving
with the sounds
of our desperate,
mule-like braying.

The Sea Glass Ghost

My fin is mighty,
but I am small
and the waves wear
away at me and
I become sea glass.

Make the mermaid smaller.
Make the mermaid smoother,
    more malleable,
    more docile,
        until she is a wisp,
        until she disappears
            and becomes another aimless ghost
            wandering the beach.

Chipped Rocks

Shards of rocks may sound like strange company,
    but they sound like perfect company to
        the mermaid with the clam ear.

The chipped rocks listen.
    I find faces in their nooks.
        I find faces in their crags.

What a stoic but attentive audience.

Going About 99

Shadows from the lace curtains cut your face into one hundred black lilies. You were in our bed, propped up too close to the fogged up window. Your mother had embroidered the satin pillow that made it possible for you to sit up because your body no longer could. Your muscles had all the strength of a toadstool trying to bolster a boulder. I didn't mind that the bed smelled musty because you had spent the last week dying in it. But I *did* mind that your bones pushed through your yellow skin more and more each day. You had always been a substantial woman.

When we first fucked, I took comfort in the depths of your flesh. From there, we made love. Sometimes, we made love hard and rough, but we still made love. I adored every pound of you. Friends accused me of having a fetish.

"What's her fetish then? Skinny blonde bitches?" I quipped.

"No, that's what everyone wants," they said while sipping their margaritas at the only lesbian bar in town. "That can't be a fetish."

I told them that the reason their pussies were dry was because they had hearts of stone.

"Why are you so desperate? You could have anyone."

"I'm desperate for her because she's the one I want."

Somehow, I had convinced myself that you didn't want me. I felt certain that I wasn't smart enough. You managed a prestigious archive at a university library while I hosted at a steakhouse downtown. Academics across the country interviewed you for journals and books from elite presses. Meanwhile, I could barely remember to give menus to the flocks of tobacco corporation executives who came to my workplace every day. You had discipline; I had dreams.

But if I hadn't been bumbling my way through another dead-end job in the city that gave my pathetic little suburb the right to exist, I never would've met you.

"Table for one," you crooned as you marched up to my stand. The harmony of your voice intrigued me, especially since it came from such plush, red lips. You were sharply dressed in a black cocktail dress and Kit Kat Club glasses to match. But it was the shock of pink hair that hooked me.

"One?"

"Yes, just me tonight."

It was 2000 and I had been out all year. Just two years before you walked into that smoky steakhouse, the press outed George Michael after an undercover police officer found him having sex in a public restroom. Humiliated, he admitted that he was gay in a national CNN interview.

As a 23-year-old Baptist from the outskirts of Richmond, Virginia, I was not supposed to fall in love with you. I was supposed to fall in love with a weak-chinned boy from school or church and be married by now. Where was my ring? Where was my child?

"Would you like a table or a booth?"

"Oh," you said, slightly startled, but quick to chuckle. "Well, a booth then!"

"What brings you here tonight?"

"Nothing special. I'm a regular. I like the skirt steak."

"I've never seen you here before."

You raised your powdered eyebrows.

"I just mean we get so many businessmen. I think I would notice...a woman like you."

We were standing at your table when you looked straight at me and said, "You mean a lesbian?" You laughed it off, but when you later told me you were testing your gaydar, I was flattered.

"Yeah, I guess," I laughed, embarrassed. I pulled out your chair and set down the menu. "Enjoy your meal."

Maybe our history might have ended with our encounter at table no. 7, but I found your note later that night. You had scrawled *Do you like comics?* with your name and number on a napkin. Best yet, you had written it in metallic purple gel pen. Even before I came out, I knew I wanted a woman with style.

"Panache," you later corrected me. You were fingering me in the back of the archives that had become your life's work when you whispered that in my ear. Somehow, you had singlehandedly persuaded thousands of comic geeks from across the country to donate their rare editions to the university library. In less than a decade, you had taken the collection from literally one title to the largest university comic book collection in the United States. All this before age 35.

You were bragging, but I didn't mind. I wanted you to talk

to me, to hold me, to run your fingers through my hair. I felt more electricity making out with you among those comic books than I did losing my virginity to Robby Stone the night of my junior prom. The latter had been my hetero test and I failed it. I wept for a month. To this day, I hate Camaros.

As you lay in our bed dying, I recalled the former roundness of your belly and how I took solace in it. You let me cry there until my mascara ran down my cheeks and I resembled the raccoons that terrorized my grandpa's old apple farm in the holler. You said your weight came from all the cornbread that your mama made you when you were growing up in Charlotte.

Once you ended your cancer treatment, the doctor told me that you were almost too delicate to touch.

"I've touched a lot of ancient paper in the past sixteen years, doc. That's what happens when you marry a librarian."

He smiled, but didn't say anything.

I touched you, anyway. I didn't rest my head on your belly because you had no belly to speak of, but I did hold your hand. I stroked your sunken cheeks. I even rubbed lotion on your skeletal feet. I touched you as gently as I knew possible. I looked after you in ways the nurses could not.

Of course, there was no one to look after me. Even with in-home hospice care, the nurses must call it a day and return to their personal lives. We had no children and, apparently, no true friends. While plenty of people were happy to take part in our wedding, none of them could be bothered to comfort me or even relieve me from simple household chores. One goddamn casserole was too much to ask. The burden of carrying out the most mundane tasks while the love of my life was dying fell completely and totally on me. I accepted that I couldn't rely on my homophobic, racist family, but what about my friends? Where was the so-called LGBTQ community? Where were my flag-waving, oh-so-open-minded allies? When I actually needed them, they could not be bothered.

Once the shift nurse went home, it was just the two of us. The first couple of nights, I attempted to fall asleep once the nurse left, but I could never squeeze in more than a nap before I woke up shrieking. I was terrified that you would die while I slept. So instead, I read to you until you fell asleep. At this stage, you could no longer sleep peacefully. Even though it pained me to watch you twitch and even kick in your feebleness, I kept my eyes on you. These moments were part of the countdown.

I could usually stand these periods of obsessive observation for about an hour. Then I had to pour myself a drink. It always started with one, but it could never end there. One drink became two and two became three and three became four and then I typically lost count. You knew when you married me that I had an addictive personality. You were just always there to temper it. Normally, you would cajole me to bed and I no longer cared for another drink. My desire for you ignited every vein, every pore, every hair on my body. I would follow you to bed, knowing in my bones that you going down on me would give me a much bigger buzz than that next gin and tonic ever could.

Yet once you entered hospice care, you could not supervise or seduce me. Alcohol entertained me until it drowned my brains. I needed to drown them so I could forget that we would not grow old together. We would never venture to Paris or Australia together. We would never eat chicken quesadillas at our favorite drive-thru or catch another dollar movie at our go-to dollar movie theater. We would never make love ever again. I wanted to taste your cunt until you squealed and moaned. I wanted to kiss you until you teared up and giggled and cried.

But I couldn't do much more than watch you.

The doctor had practically wrapped you up in caution tape.

On that seventh night of hospice care, I told myself that this was not how you wanted to live and this was not how you wanted to die. I cannot say how many drinks I'd had by then, only that I'd had more than any good Baptist girl was supposed to have. Needless to say, I was not a "good" Baptist girl. I wasn't even a bad Baptist girl. I was a godless girl and I was not sorry for it. I was sorry for not loving you harder. I was sorry that I could not inhale you and possess you or even become you. I wanted to preserve you. I wanted to protect you. I wanted to take all of the faith I did not have in religion and put it in you.

When I left church life for good, we had been dating shy of three months. I swore that I no longer believed in God, but I didn't invest that belief elsewhere. I believed in you in the sense that I supported you. But you were in your early 30s and had already accomplished so much. How much of my support did you really need? I doubted our relationship needed my faith, either. I took it for granted that we sustained each other. For that reason, I didn't think our relationship needed faith. I should've believed in the power of us as much as I had once believed in the power of God. Even atheists need faith in something.

You were still doing your end-of-life equivalent of tossing and turning when I appeared at your side in my wedding dress. It shone scarlet in the lamplight. I discovered the iridescent gown at a disco vintage shop and wore it to the courthouse with twinning silk shoes. You had on the same cocktail dress you were wearing when we met. I had talked you into donning a daisy crown all through the ceremony and reception. It's poignant to think that your black father and white mother were lucky to meet after the U.S. Supreme Court legalized interracial marriage. We met 14 years before gay marriage was legalized, but it wasn't too late for us. We could still walk down that aisle.

I poked you because I wanted you to wake up and see me in my wedding dress. I wanted you to remember how beautiful I had been when we got married. Somehow, in my drunkenness, I had even approximated the big beauty queen hair I wore on our wedding day. It wasn't exactly a flawless recreation, but I knew you would get the idea.

I poked you again when you would not wake up. Aware that your sleep was not a deep one, I figured one poke would be enough to wake you. It was not. It took half a dozen prods to rouse you. Though your body remained stiff, you gradually fluttered open your hazel eyes. I couldn't tell what color your eyes were when we first met because you had on glasses and the steakhouse was so dim. But on our first date, we were outside of a coffee shop in the light of day, discussing *Superman* and *Little Audrey*. Sometime during your telling of Lois Lane's feminist revolution, I noticed that your eyes were pools of light brown with green and gray flecks. It was during that same conversation that you got me to admit that I wanted to be an illustrator.

You didn't have much control of your facial expressions in this final phase, so I read your eyes. It took a few beats, but your eyes lit up when you registered that I had on my wedding dress. I almost tricked myself into thinking that you had turned. You weren't going to die. You'd recover. You'd survive. We could go to Paris and Australia and the chicken quesadilla place and the dollar movie theater.

Then you coughed.

"No!" I shouted. It was the biggest noise the house had heard all week. I clamped my hands over my mouth. "I'm sorry," I whispered. "I won't be that loud again. I'll put on some Nat King Cole—real soft, promise."

"Unforgettable," which we played for our first dance, eked from my iPod. The song had never sounded so slow before. But as you lay there, it played slowly and softly for you. Too drunk to mimic our first dance, I simply twirled.

This is the when the alcohol began making waves in my skull. It wouldn't be the first time you saw me stumbling drunk, but it would be the last time. I always used to say that you were my weakness. While that was true, my fixation on you never hurt me the way my slavish dependence on gin hurt me. You encouraged me to draw, to pour out the contents of my imagination on the page. You encouraged me to abandon the church that made me miserable. You encouraged me to embrace my sexuality. All you ever did was encourage me, except when it came to drinking. That was one desire of mine you were eager to stifle.

I'm not sure how long I was twirling, but I could not spin around and around forever. I got dizzy and collapsed into the rocking chair that held my iPod. I thought the crunching noise came from my bones hitting the wood at the wrong angle. That wasn't it. I had crushed the iPod. It was gone. Done. I threw the iPod's remains against the wall and wailed.

Your beauteous hazel eyes had closed again, so I came over to rub your forehead.

"Wake up, my love," I said.

You did not wake up.

"Wake up," I growled. "Wake up. Wake up."

I shook you by the shoulders and you woke up. Maybe I should've seen the terror in your eyes and stopped, but I did not. Instead, I kissed you. I knew I was not supposed to kiss you, at least not with any real vigor—any real feeling—but I did. You could not reciprocate. Your tongue remained curled up in your dry, dying mouth. Your once bee-stung lips were parched.

If I could not kiss you, I figured I could hold you. Thus, I violated another one of the doctor's orders. I swept you up in my arms and cradled you. One year ago, I could not have possibly done that. For fifteen out of our sixteen years together, you dwarfed me. Now I was the big one, the strong one.

If you responded to me cradling you, I did not notice. As much as I loathe admitting it, the night was no longer about you. It was about me. Alcohol had made it about me. By drinking, I had made the night about me. It's tempting to wonder whose brain was more alive then—yours or mine.

I kicked off my heels and stood up with you still in my arms. I stopped marveling at how light you were. Now, it was a fact, just like the fact that you were dying. I couldn't be stunned forever. The novelty of this new reality had worn off and my perception adjusted accordingly.

Maybe that is why I began heading toward our pool. It glowed in the backyard, calling to me as it had in all of our years hosting lesbian pool parties. Our email invitations always read "No boys allowed." Funny how friends will come to your Southside house to enjoy your pool, but none of them will come to your Southside house to mow your lawn or do your laundry when your wife is dying.

The pool hadn't only been for parties. Really, it was for us. Sometimes we'd read in our beach chairs and just stare at it as the water lapped the steps. Other times we'd play volleyball or swim laps. The sensation of underwater sex never lost its appeal, either.

Even in my drunken state, I knew we would not play volleyball or swim laps. Sex, too, was out of the question. But I saw no harm in us floating in our inflatable pool raft shaped like a Corvette. It was as pink as your hair had been at our wedding.

Maneuvering into the raft with you in my arms was no problem. For thirty seconds, I seemed to regain my sense of balance. I held you tight and, sometime while floating, I fell asleep.

You and I almost died once during the first year of our relationship. All of the downtown bars were closed, but you insisted on going into the city anyway. You were almost certain that this one diner was still open. Those were the pre-Internet days and you saw no point in calling, so we had to drive there to find out. When we approached the James River Bridge, you let out a battle cry and hit the gas. It was clear at 3 a.m., which made the fact that you were going about 99 a little less unforgivable. Still, I was horrified.

That horror increased tenfold when a homeless man toppled into the street. You swerved to miss him, momentarily losing control of the car. You just missed a lamppost as we ricocheted from one side of the bridge to the other and then shot down the length of it into Richmond.

"We made it!" you yelled, a crazed grin taking up more than half of your face.

I sat in silence for a full minute before confessing that we needed to go home because I shat my pants.

We could not have possibly been going 99 in our Corvette raft when I woke up. Yet we had been going fast enough— or at least clumsily enough—that you had fallen off of the raft. I didn't realize it at first because I didn't understand why I was in the pool. I didn't know where I was and I couldn't remember why I had on my wedding dress. What I did know was that I had been clutching you like the most precious jewel on earth because that's exactly what you were to me. But I had let you go. I deduced this because you were facedown in the water.

This was not a nightmare. This was my life, which had somehow escalated past the terror of any nightmare I had ever had. After days of forcing myself to stay awake for your last breath, I had been asleep when you died.

I paddled the raft over to you and scooped you up. It was only then, holding you as the Blessed Mother held Christ, that I howled. Otherwise, I did not move.

I am still in this raft with you in my arms, not knowing what I will tell the police, though I swear I will call them at sunrise. All I do know is that I will never drink again or draw again or love again. I could say that it was your greatness that has made such things impossible, but really, it is my worthlessness. When you told me that I was worthy, you were lying. I am less than the scum sticking to the sides of our pool, your deathbed.

One-armed Starfish

Tidal pools bear gifts.

Tidal pools bear temporary company.

Tidal pools sometimes bear one-armed starfish,

    broken like me,

    incomplete like me.

I greet her, pick her up, and rub her stump.

Then I return her to the placid water

    and rub my clam ear

    while contemplating the sea,

      the angry, choppy sea.

Winter has no mercy for the lonely.

Shells and Corpses and Spirits

Collecting seashells reminds me of
all the creatures that have died
and returned to the ocean
as salt and minerals and ghosts.

If this shell is a tombstone,
does that make me a gravedigger
or a grave robber?

My basket overflows with
nods to corpses and spirits.

Who is nodding?
I am nodding.
I want to resurrect the dead,
but breathing life into something
requires beauty and strength
and I have neither.

The Mermaid and the Merman

I am bound to the boardwalk, even
with snowflakes piercing the air.

I am terrified of going home,
of staring into a fireplace
filled with desperate flames that
will burn forever.

I am terrified of going home,
of staring at an empty dinner table
and realizing that I am always alone.

But then I notice a man on the boardwalk.
He looks out at the icy sea
and then up at the swirling snowflakes
before sighing the
most ancient sounding of sighs.

We could dive into the terrible waves together
and calm the raging waters with our love.
Maybe we are meant for a life beyond the boardwalk.
Maybe we are meant to inhabit a coral castle
and never doubt our place among the squids and fish.

We can catch the snowflakes.
We can melt the ice.
First, we must catch each other's eye
and speak true and simple words
that conquer the heart without deception.
The ocean has no room for lies.

Love Among the Frail

I spy upon the merman
as he returns to the cove,
gray day after gray day,
always alone.
He has a thin harelip
unlike any man in the village.
It harkens my clam ear
in its frailty.
I wonder if he passes the time
collecting frail things
to keep him company
by the cold sea.
I know I have done the same.
Is it safe for me to approach him?
Or will he crumble like a sand castle
in the gustiest of winter winds?
Perhaps the lonely mermaid is
destined to love
the lonely merman
from afar.

The Disappearing Clam Ear

The more I fell in love with the merman,
the more my clam ear disappeared.
Instead of fixating on my deformity,
I fixated on my undulating heart rate.
My body could beat so fast
and then freeze into an iceberg,
growing puffins and polar bears
in some far-off northern sea.
I would heat up and sweat
before cooling down and shivering.
Love is so hot and love is so cold.

Yet my beloved would continue
combing the beach unchanged,
unaware of my watching,
unaware of my pining,
unaware of my heating up,
unaware of my cooling down,
unaware that he seized my mind
and transformed my worldview
when all he did was jostle
a few grains of sand.

My Inner Sea Witch

Your inner dialogue:

Put a spell on the merman.
You have the power
to crush a scallop shell,
ground two barnacles,
pluck a sea gull feather,
and not regret it.
You smash your ego
all the time.

The aim of the spell
is achingly simple:
to make him love you.
It is not impossible.
But maybe you don't
need a spell.
Not that you aren't
capable of casting one.
You could talk
to him instead.
Snare him with
your words,
your ideas,
your laugh.

The mermaid and
the merman
are meant to be.
No magic required.

Se llamaba Mariposa

The drought in Jalisco may have preoccupied me more if the thought of coming out to my parents hadn't held my brain hostage. "Drought" became the jaguar in the cornfields, the toxic toupee on a twig. Jalisco hadn't tasted rain in days. Los jalicienses hissed and brayed and howled that it had rained less and less every spring for years.

I had spent the earlier part of the evening boozing up on bathtub gin and digging through people's garbage. Hoping for stuff to resell, I lucked out on unearthing a stack of black and white nudies. Most of the subjects were luchadores wrestling each other into sexual submission. The softcore stuff featured Gene Simmons-style tongue wags and macho ass grabs. The harder stuff was all about masked blowjobs and butt-fucking in costume. Lucha libre at its gayest.

I stumbled home to stash the photos under my bed to later list online. My teaching stipend was running low and someone had a fetish for the pictures that could only amuse me. Last week, it had been brand name baby formula days away from its expiration date. Another time, it was designer penny loafers with double monk straps. People toss out kingdoms of crap.

From my bed, I went to the bathroom and splashed my face with cold water. It was a steamy night with no promise of letting up. I tamed my hair by stiffening it with gel. Then I pulled off my stinky T-shirt and put on a black wife beater before slinking into the night.

There was a club in la Colonia Arcos Vallarta where you could sin any day of the week. It was as much my watering hole as it was my cesspool—that is, if five times makes a habit. I claimed a high top table in a dark corner and scanned the crowd for someone I liked. There were as many women as there were types. They pulsated beneath the starburst LEDs, purred over pool tables, pressed into the bar or each other.

"What's your name?" came a gravely voice, speaking in Spanish but with no hint of the regional accent. I glanced up from my fingernails, which I had been picking at for a good minute, all of the club's sounds and stimuli faded into background noise. I found myself in the company of a statuesque woman a decade my senior. Her eyelids were weighed down by turquoise eye shadow. I liked her toned, shiny arms.

"Makayla," I said.

She pointed at herself and breathed "Mariposa" as she draped herself over the table. "Where are you from?"

"The United States."

"Of course," she laughed and the disco lights danced off her big teeth, "but where?"

"Waynesboro, Virginia." My mind flickered to the Blue Ridge, the Civil War markers, and the P. Buckley Moss Museum. There was no Arco Iris in Waynesboro.

Mariposa nodded as a distant look came over her. "Virginia," she said very slowly, drawing out the last syllable long enough to form a new word in the Spanish language. "I lived in North Carolina for a year, a long time ago. Before you were born. I fell in love with someone from Raleigh." The way she pronounced 'Raleigh,' it rhymed with 'Olé.'

Mariposa adjusted her wig and studied my face. "Have you been there?"

I shook my head. "I never left Virginia before I came here."

"That was how it was with me and Oaxaca before I went to Raleigh."

Suddenly, Mariposa went from nostalgic to melancholy, but she emerged from her black cave of memories just as quickly as she had fallen into it. She bolted up, clapped, and shook her broad shoulders.

"Can I buy you a drink?" she asked.

I grinned a little too widely and said, "Para todo mal, mezcal, y para todo bien también."

One drink became too many drinks and soon, Mariposa and I were sitting by ourselves on the upper patio because the club beats hurt my head. I preferred to commune with the snails and marigolds.

After a few moments of silence, Mariposa said, "No one back home knows about you."

"What do you mean?"

"They don't know you're gay."

My eyes drifted from her face to the wall. "When did you tell?"

"I never told," Mariposa sighed and stood up, outstretching her arms. "I showed. But even once my transition is complete, I still will have spent 41 years living as what most people still consider a man." She closed her eyes long enough to fall asleep until I leaned over and kissed her. When she didn't reciprocate, I withdrew. I had imagined us kissing with the force of a Guadalajara storm, sucking the pain from each other's souls, but she didn't share the same fantasy.

Then it rained.

We almost didn't notice until we heard shouting in the streets. That's when we ran to the lower patio and peered down the alley. Clubbers joined abuelitas in celebration. The drought had ended. Mariposa grabbed my hand and we ran out to dance with strangers. We jumped and splashed until my body gave in. I collapsed into Mariposa's arms and muttered, "I have to go. My first class starts early tomorrow."

Mariposa nodded and hailed a taxi. She squeezed my hand as I boarded the taxi alone.

"Be safe, but not too safe," she said. Then she shut the door and the taxi took off.

When it came time to fly back to Virginia, I packed my few belongings swiftly so as not to dwell. Twelve hours later, I threw my arms around my mother and went home to have meatloaf for dinner. After dessert, I told her I was gay.

"I know," she said and patted my hand. Then, after a beat, "Why don't you load the dishwasher?"

So I did.

The Death of Self-loathing

Two bodies in the same small ship,
clinging to each other in the storm.
Fins entwined as shards of ice fly.
Once these lovers joined each other,
their deformities did not
disappear into winter's wrath,
but their self-loathing melted
from the warmth
of their hearts.
And so the mermaid
bid farewell
to her hatred
for her clam ear.

Acknowledgments

Excerpts from this book first appeared in the e-book *Lavinia Moves to New York* (Underground Voices) and the chapbooks *Harlem Mestiza* (Maverick Duck Press), *Jaguar in the Cotton Field* (Another New Calligraphy), *The Tale of the Clam Ear* (AngelHouse Press), and *Ova* (Dancing Girl Press). Thank you to Ghia Vitale for her editing expertise and to everyone at *Quail Bell Magazine* for giving me a community of writers, artists, and thinkers.

Christine Sloan Stoddard

is a Salvadoran-American author, artist, and the founder of *Quail Bell Magazine*. Her books include *Belladonna Magic: Spells In The Form of Poetry And Photography* (Shanti Arts), *Water for the Cactus Woman* (Spuyten Duyvil), *Hispanic and Latino Heritage in Virginia* (The History Press), and other titles. Her art and writing have appeared in *Ms. Magazine, The Feminist Wire, Bustle, Cosmopolitan, Native Peoples Magazine, Yes! Magazine, Teen Vogue, The Social Justice Review, Marie Claire*, and elsewhere. A graduate of VCUarts and The City College of New York-CUNY, Stoddard lives in Brooklyn with her husband and a dead cactus.